TORMENT

One Woman's Revenge

Revenge never expires in a mind that fails to sleep

LEANNE WOOD

Table of Contents

Dedication

To my gorgeous – it's a privilege to share my life and love with you. Thank you for always believing in me, for your unwavering support and constant encouragement, even on my darkest days.

Your patience and understanding helped make this book possible. Thank you for putting up with my sleepless nights, my messy office, and for reading and listening to my ever-changing versions.

You are my number 1 fan and my soul mate. I love you with all my heart, plus more.

LEANNE WOOD

PROLOGUE

Imagine if the world was perfect, free of war and hunger. How wonderful would it be to live in an environment where everyone flourished and every family was flawless? Where all mankind accepted and respected differences. Violence would not exist nor would harassment, discrimination and bullying. Resentment would be superfluous; everyone would be happy and kind. Forgiveness unnecessary as there would be nothing to forgive.

It sounds wonderful. I am sure everyone wishes it were possible. We can all dream. Yet we know this is purely an idealistic conception of reality, in essence an unattainable vision.

I remember when my opinion of life was so different; so many years have passed and so many inconceivable events have occurred. I used to think I was untouchable, indestructible. My life was brilliant. But everything can change in a blink of an eye. When I look back, it is hard to believe I am where I am today. My life was shattered, but I am no longer a victim. I am no longer broken and forever limited by my suffering. I am so much more than a survivor. So much has happened. So much has changed.

These days I possess a clear acceptance that our world is imperfect. Bad things can happen to good people, just as good things can happen to those we consider bad. Our world is flawed and full of corruption and greed. It is a place where love, acceptance and trust clash with annoyance, anger and rage. Minds are fuelled by negative feelings, which create terror, apprehension and fear. People loath others, actions disgust, sadness engulfs and grief consumes. People crumble, depression invades; acts of retaliation appear the only option. It is a world in which I believed revenge would be my saviour.

TWELVE MONTHS EARLIER

Yesterday was one of those, 'fuck this shit!' type of days. I was mentally, emotionally, and physically exhausted. For too long my days had been filled with mammoth fails and micro victories. Getting out of bed was an effort. Opening the front blinds was something I had not yet achieved. People told me to get over it – life was for living and I should move forward. Why couldn't I just forget about the past? But things are sometimes easier said than done. The only place I felt safe was within the confines of my home. Blinds closed, curtains drawn, hidden from attack. Horrifying thoughts plagued my waking hours, haunting flashbacks and nightmares made sleep impossible. I felt like I was going crazy. Would there ever be an end to the unrelenting turmoil?

It had been seven years, three months and five days since I left Wolf Industries. Hard to believe so much time had passed. The place was a nightmare. If I could erase that section of my life, I would. My life was pretty well fucked. I had no reason for living. No purpose. I no longer resembled the confidant, smart and carefree person I was before that hell hole. If I knew then what I know now, I never would have stepped foot in the place. It should be burnt to the ground. Work for Wolf Industries and you will never be the same; maybe they should put that as a warning on their job application.

Yet the place still exists; employees come and go – after all, everyone needs to work and Wolf Industries employs hundreds. So while it powers into its future, I remain trapped by my past.

That is… I was trapped.

Last night, my partner of ten years, Zack, announced he was leaving. He'd had enough. Labelling me a 'nutcase' and 'volatile', he said I belonged in a loony bin.

I can't say his leaving was unexpected; our relationship had been crumbling for some time. He was sick of me, and I was sick of his 'get over it' attitude. His leaving will be a blessing. Now I will have my freedom. He said he could no longer take the pressure of my 'unpredictable mental state'. He claimed I had introduced chaos into his life. It was easier for him to blame me than to be a man and admit he had fallen for Sandra, the office slut. Sandra 'Suckadick' Wilson had been after Zack for as long as I could remember. I had met her years earlier at one of his work functions – the bleach-blonde bimbo covered in layers of fake tan, willing to spread her legs for career advancement. Zack couldn't see it, but he would soon discover his involvement with her would only extend to satisfy her needs. I hoped she wasn't under the assumption these needs would be fulfilled between the sheets. Zack's sexual prowess wasn't as good as he led himself to believe.

I could have shattered his ego had I told him the truth about our sex life – I had been faking orgasms for years. That screeching escaping my lips was definitely not due to my being at the peak of my sexual excitement while he had been 'working his magic'. Before I became ill I would generally drift into thoughts about daily tasks, people I had to see, places I needed to go, and a lot of the time I would prepare our shopping list. By the time my thoughts had moved up and down the supermarket aisles, he was done and I was approaching the cash register realising how much the groceries were going to cost. *"Uhhh, uhhh, ahhh!"*

After I got sick our sex life became virtually non-existent. A side effect of my prescribed medication was significant weight gain resulting in further thoughts of worthlessness. The stigma surrounding mental health was devastating. 'Friends' left in droves. I tried to mask my depression with alcohol; I popped pills in an attempt to block out all feelings and to sleep. The thought of having sex repulsed me. I became despondent, withdrawn, emotional and at my lowest point, suicidal. Zack's announcement propelled me into overwhelming blackness. I felt nothing.

I watched, unmoving, as he packed his bags; listened calmly as he laid claim to different articles around the house. There was no need for an argument. I wasn't about to admit I was worried how I would cope. When he looked in my direction, I acknowledged his statements with a smile and a nod, not paying attention to his words. And finally, when he closed the front door behind him, I cheered.

Three months. I would give him three months to come back and collect the rest of his things. After that they would be out on the footpath. Suckadick could have him. I was free.

Last night I went to bed alone and a victim of my past. This morning I rise a warrior.

Too much time has been wasted. If I don't get off my backside now I never will. And they will win. Those at Wolf Industries who did me wrong will continue as if nothing has happened. I will be a footnote in a bad joke. One day I will die and be forgotten. I can't let them get away with it. My mind is set. I need no sympathy. I require no words. Today I am a woman with purpose. My mission is payback.

If I can't forget, then neither will they. Circumstances can change at any time, and I will show them that without warning victims can evolve into far more than survivors. They will learn the hunter can become the hunted. For I can no longer wait for things to get easier, simpler or better. It is their time to wake up to the living, breathing hell I have had to face. There will be no turning back.

Call it a moment of clarity, call it stupidity – this is my

journey and I will not be deterred. My past will no longer restrict and suffocate me, nor will it control my future. My anger has grown limbs of its own. Deep-rooted hatred towards my attackers branch out into thoughts of revenge. In-depth logistical strategies and systematic schemes distract me from my turmoil and offer a glimmer of hope. For I haven't just planned, I have plotted my revenge against those who destroyed my life.

There are four. Four that will fall. Fuck them.

Fuck them all.

I pull back the curtains and stare at the closed blinds. A flutter of fear in my gut, but I welcome my challenge. *Good morning revenge.*

Pacing the kitchen, my anxiety begins to peak. Sweat covers my brow. A nervous energy makes me tremble. The room instantly fell cold. I need to see my therapist. A sense of urgency takes hold; I must keep the momentum of my thoughts alive. It is imperative I tell someone I can trust about my exciting new revelation. I know he will be happy for me. I know Daniel will share in my joy. I sit at the kitchen table. My fingers tap its wooden surface. I am in the silence of my thoughts. Doubt enters. I hope he will share my joy. Surely he will share it with me.

CHAPTER ONE

Bridget Tilner's drive to therapy would take ten minutes. Two sets of traffic lights, four roundabouts, no school zones or pedestrian crossings – minimal exposure. The doors to her car would be locked. The windows were tinted and would remain closed. The radio volume would be set high. She only needed to focus on the road ahead and listen to the music. Music was a great distraction. Her sunglasses and hat would aid in her disguise.

Long, determined strides propelled her to her front door – an area she had steered clear of for some time. Heart racing, her mind was set. She wrapped her hand around the door handle. The coolness of the brass brought everything into sharp focus. She shuddered as she glanced towards the front window to the right of the door. The timber blinds remained closed. Her hand remained fixed to the door, and her mind yelled at her to retreat. It would be so much easier to remain inside her home where it was safe. Heart pounding, she sucked in a large breath. *Why is this so difficult?* Now she's pissed off. She could not let them beat her. Closing her eyes, she reassured herself the only way forward was forward. As stupid as it sounded, forward was difficult when one has been existing in a holding pattern for such a long time. She could no longer allow the demons control.

With a slight twist of her wrist the door opened and the

warmth of the sun greeted her. It felt good. She sucked in another deep breath and assured herself all would be fine. Her therapist had spoken about desensitisation, distraction and living in the moment. No bolts of lightning had struck her dead, if she focused on her breath and her mission at hand then surely all would be fine. A slight sweat covered her brow. Her eyes scanned the street; her ears pricked for danger signs. An electric saw rang out. She assumed it is came from two doors down. From between the slithered gaps in the kitchen blinds she'd noticed trades people coming and going for the past two weeks. A skip bin was perched on their front lawn. *Renovations*. Strange cars and people always made her nervous.

Nausea hit her hard, churning deep within her gut. *I'm going to be sick..* A lump formed within her throat. She swallowed back bile. The bitterness lingered. Her hands were warm and clammy. Her head starts to pound. Buzzing filled her ears. The world begins to spin. The warmth that settled on her face only moments ago had vanished. The air was now thick and cold. She sucked in short breaths. Every part of her shook uncontrollably. Grabbing the wooden door frame she attempted to steady herself. Her hands were weak. Her fingers numb. *This is bullshit. You're a fucken loser.*

She turned quickly and stumbled, slamming the door behind her as she made her retreat. *Safe.* Bridget collapsed on the floor. Torrents of tears escaped her eyes. "Fuck them, fuck them all," she sobbed. Fear was in control. She hated herself. Despised her reactions. Why couldn't she just get over it?

Five minute passed, then five more. Her breathing settled, yet her upset remains. She seriously could not let them win. She needed to do this. She needed to leave her house. How would she exact revenge if she couldn't even leave her house? *This is ridiculous. I am ridiculous.* No wonder they picked her as a target of their bullying and harassment. 'Soft cock' was one title bestowed upon her. How could a woman be a soft cock? Disgusting. What type of man felt proud for picking on a woman? All the titles they'd doled out swirled through her: loser, fucktard, bitch, Adolf Titler, thundercunt, skittle tits. There were so many. That her name was Bridget aided in their taunts – build a *bridge* and *get* over it. Oh how they'd laughed. So many vulgar titles. So many hateful attacks. Why? Why had they singled her out?

Tears streamed down her face and washed away her sadness and anger, leaving a clear path for the return of her determination. She couldn't let them win. She wouldn't. Her determination returned. She had nothing to lose. No one understood the invisibility of mental illness. There were no physical injuries or scars, but it had the propensity to silently kill. Fear controlled and restricted. It suffocated whether the threat was real or imagined. *Now or never.*

She needed to speak to Daniel, her therapist. He would reassure her. His gentle and caring nature was something she had come to rely upon. She trusted him. His kind words always offered hope.

It took twenty-seven minutes and two more attempts before she was successfully in her car and on her way to therapy. A huge improvement from what she had been able to achieve. Twelve months ago she would have been up vomiting for hours before she'd even attempted to open the front door. Her nerves had been so shattered that she stuttered under pressure.

In the car her windows remained closed and her doors were locked. She double-checked them while driving. She was relieved her next appointment with Daniel was this morning. She needed to talk to him about her plan. Talking helped. Every word that passed her lips within therapy remained confidential. He would understand. He was the only one who understood. He would know what to do. She would show him the list of four names scrawled on the back of an old shopping docket.

Samuel Easton would be the first.

CHAPTER TWO

Walking into the therapist's office, Bridget was both nervous and excited. The air seemed thick and weighty, but her hopes were high. Daniel Priest had been her therapist for over seven years. He had seen her at her worst. Daniel was her saviour; he understood where she was coming from and did not set unrealistic expectations. Bridget called him her angel – an angel with a perfectly symmetrical face. To her, he was a guardian and protector. He listened and did not cast aspersions. In his late forties, he'd been a practising psychiatrist for all his working life. A kind-hearted soul Bridget had become reliant upon. So much so she sometimes questioned her feelings. She knew he liked her. He'd said he always looked forward to her appointments. She could trust him with her inner most secrets.

Daniel knew all about Bridget, even that she hadn't enjoyed sex with Zack but had felt compelled to stay with him. Daniel was her lifeline; the voice of reason. The first time they had met he had eased her mind, offered hope. She vowed then she would always trust him, to listen and heed his advice. He was a wise man and extremely good looking. *He can press my buttons any day.*

Sitting in the waiting room, Bridget smiled nervously at Hilary, Daniel's receptionist. Hilary appeared close to retiring age. Her voice was husky yet harmonic. Her silver hair was neat and likely styled with old-fashioned rollers. Wispy strands and tight curls framed her world-weary face, and deep lines danced around her eyes and mouth as she spoke. It was only when she stood from behind the reception desk that you noticed her bent back. It was as if she carried with her all the invisible weights of the world. A steady shuffle took her between the filing cabinet and copying machine. Bridget wondered if she had always been this way or had her aged shuffle replaced a youthful march. But it would be rude to ask. Scanning the waiting room she wondered if Daniel would be pleased with her latest revelations. She prayed he would acknowledge the positivity behind her plans. *An eye for an eye.*

Finally the office door opened and Bridget was greeted by Daniel's welcoming smile. He looked better than when she had last seen him. His slightly wavy brown hair was slicked back, his face freshly shaven. She looked him up and down and returned a smile. Today he was wearing his grey and snug fitting dress pants with perfectly ironed seams, a black leather belt, a white business shirt and his lavender silk tie. Bridget had given Daniel the tie as a Christmas present two years ago. She was thrilled he wore it and she loved it when he wore those pants. She could imagine every bulging bit. *One silk tie, a leather belt and you absent of those snug pants could work wonders for my recovery,* she thought as she brushed passed him. Sauntering over to the corner of the room she flopped down onto the chair. She always sat in the corner. No vacant space was allowed behind. It was imperative she see all aspects of the room. Daniel locked the door. He reached over and turned on his desk lamp then the tripod lamp, which sat to the right of the door. Bridget admired the way he stretched and walked. Even fully dressed she could tell he took pride in keeping fit. His body was toned. His strides were confident. The curtains were drawn. It was a regimented routine. Only when all these requirements were fulfilled was she able to relax. A patient needed to be comfortable to speak freely.

Daniel sat in his chair and lent forward, he crossed his arms and rested them on his desk.

"How are you Bridget? You look well," he smiled.

"I am well and I have so much to tell you Daniel. So much has happened since we last saw each other." She took a breath then blurted, "Zack left me, he says I am a whacko." Pausing for a moment she examined Daniel's reaction. His raised eyebrows could mean anything.

"Are you okay?" he asked, letting out a ragged breath while running his hands through his hair.

"Yep, I am actually better than okay. You see I have a plan. A recovery plan…"

Daniel remained silent, his head tilted slightly as he waited to hear more.

Squirming around in her chair Bridget began to inhale deeply. Her lips twitched. Her eyes scanned the room. She rose to her feet and began pacing in front of his desk.

"No one understands the effect bullying and harassment can have on a person. One day you are waking up looking forward to a productive and enjoyable workday. Before you know it you wake up filled with dread and fear of what will happen." She battled to maintain her composure as she clenched her hands. "My happiness was stripped. I broke down easily. I began to stutter. I barely slept and I began to overthink everything. Everyone could be an enemy. I was guarded, walls went up, and I withdrew from the world. My trust evaporated. My paranoia increased. Haunting nightmares invaded. Their behaviour was so vicious and insidious."

Bridget suddenly paused then slammed her fists I onto Daniel's desk. She gazed down at him. He sat still in his black high-backed leather chair, his feet firmly planted on the ground, hands clasped gently on his lap. His brow was furrowed in concern, his lips closed as he listened to her every word. It was important for a victim to speak, she knew that. Vocalising was a part of releasing the pain he'd told her; it didn't matter that he'd heard the words before. The important thing was that she could release, release and release until release was no longer required. Only when the need to release had passed would she sit and accept her pain without the all-consuming sadness, guilt and dread.

When Bridget first came to him for help her words had been limited. Guilt for being so weak had overwhelmed her. She would sit on the chair rocking back and forth, a blubbering mess. Sobbing incessantly. He would offer tissues to wipe away her tears. Discarded tissues piled high in the trash by the time her therapy session concluded. The road ahead would be long and challenging.

Releasing a loud sigh Bridget shook her head, squeezed her eyes tightly closed and flicked her hands. Her heart pounded. Her frustration peaked. But his silence only urged her to speak – they both knew this path well.

"I feared reprisals for taking a stand. I faked the smiles. I hid the pain. I continued to lodge complaints. I hated getting out of bed in the morning. I feared going to work. People asked why I just didn't leave, but why should I? I loved my job, I needed to work, and no person should be forced out of his or her employment," she said as her voice raised. She paused and stared into nothingness. Tears filled her eyes. She wiped her face and took a deep breath. "A wild animal should be kept within a contained environment. A bully should be controlled within a workplace. My employer should have protected me, but they didn't. They, too, are responsible. They did nothing. They stood idly by. My attempting to seem unaffected got harder and harder. Reporting threats appeared useless but I continued. Can't you see? I'm still hurting. I can't tell my story without bursting into tears." She shook her head. "My physical scars have disappeared but the memories remain. It was mental torture every day. *Every. Day.* I couldn't sleep for worrying what would happen next. Others took Pierre's side for fear of being picked on themselves. Some found it amusing. I've been to hell and back. It's always there, lurking behind me. I look out while the monsters look in. I am trapped in my own mind forever. They're right behind me. Always. The wind carries their voices. They come from the darkness, and that darkness is alive and hungry." She looked into his eyes. "I have nothing left to lose. It's funny what that can make you do," Bridget said, before turning and collapsing onto the chair in the corner. She buried her face in her hands.

Daniel sat still as he always did, allowing her time.

When her sobbing subsided, it was his time to talk. "Your past may shape your future, but your mind determines your actions," he replied, his voice calm and reassuring.

"My mind…" Bridget snapped, then paused and chuckled. Tears streamed down her cheeks but nothing would wash away her determination. "Some people would say I've lost my mind. Maybe that could be my defence. I don't know, I don't know much anymore, but I do know one thing – I have been waiting for the right time but there is no right time. There's just now. Time to jump off that hamster wheel," she said, trying to gauge his reaction. "I can no longer allow the sadness to descend, the misery to consume or the haunting flashbacks to invade. I can't live like this anymore. Something needs to change. Sometimes you have to lose everything to find out what's worth fighting for. I've lost my identity, and so it's time to create a new one. I'm telling you now, they won't know what hit them."

Silence enveloped the room.

"How? You can't be… What are you thinking?"

"I'm thinking I will make them pay," she said. "Surely you understand."

"I do, I do," Daniel said, leaning forward again. "I hear what you are saying, I know why you are saying it, but…"

"Don't you turn against me," Bridget said with a snarl. "You're either on my side or theirs," she snarled.

"I am not on their side," he said firmly. "I am here for you.

I want what is best for you."

"Then why can't you be happy for me?"

"I *am* happy for you, your new found determination is a step in the right direction but I fear your enthusiasm for revenge will end up with you behind bars. I mean, seriously who are you after? What do you plan to do?"

Bridget gaped at Daniel; his look of concern had been replaced by a blank stare.

"You know who I have in my sights, those bullying bastards who ruined my life," she said. "It's time to turn the tables."

"You have to stop this Bridget," he snapped. "I don't want to see you locked up for the rest of your life!"

Bridget shook her head then rubbed her brow before a laugh escaped her. "I won't be locked up, I'll plead insanity, diminished mental capacity, post-traumatic stress disorder, depression, anxiety… it's all in my records. Can't you see?" she said, pleading. "They can't get away with it. It's their time to suffer. I am fucken *sick* of being the only one who suffers from what they did. Why is it that I have the nightmares? Why is it that I feel so afraid and don't dare walk down the street? Why is it I feel sick when I hear their names? Why? You tell me why! Give me one good reason why they shouldn't pay for what they did to me. They're *bastards*. They were men, full grown men. Men who decided to pick on a woman. What does that make them?"

Tears welled in Bridget's eyes. When she spoke about them she transformed. Anger erupted from within. Her eyes darkened. Her face reddened. Teeth clenched. Hands fisted in rage. Within seconds tears were again streaming down her face. She cracked.

***

She was broken. *They* had broken her. Daniel was lost for

words. He stood from his chair and walked to the corner of his desk. Paused. He wanted nothing more than to embrace her, to rid her of her suffering. Any man who abused a woman was not a man at all. How could he argue with her? Their callous comments and behaviour, their total disregard for Bridget had left devastation in their wake. It was sickening. The idea of revenge was no doubt delectable. Visualising the satisfaction of bringing harm upon those, of being able to vent aggression… Maybe an act of revenge would restore balance within the moral universe and enable Bridget to find peace. He winced at the thought. Turning, he walked back to his chair shaking his head. He remained silent. Nervously looking towards Bridget he battled with what he should say. *Morality,* he thought, *who am I to question what is wrong or right? How can I argue with what a victim claims will assist in recovery – would revenge lessen her emotional pain?*

CHAPTER THREE

Monday, the first day of September, was the day Bridget was to launch her first attack. It had been three weeks since she'd seen Daniel, three weeks since she'd spoken to him. He had phoned but she hadn't answered. He knew only of her intentions. When she'd left his office she'd assured him she would give his words great consideration. Better to keep it that way. However, her determination had not swayed and in those three weeks she had dedicated her life to planning and surveillance.

Her first priority had been changing the locks to her house. Zack had been over to collect more of his clothes, but clearing out his belongings would take several more trips. He had agreed Bridget could keep the furniture and the weight bench in the garage but insisted he take full ownership of the boat they had purchased together years earlier. Bridget concurred. The boat would be transferred into his name and he would be allowed to maintain storage of it in her garage until Christmas where he would then make alternative arrangements.

Bridget was surprised at how amicable their discussions had been, but she didn't want Zack turning up unannounced and entering into what was now *her* domain. She asked that in future he message her in advance and organise a time suitable to them both before coming over again.

Everything was on track. It was all falling into place. Her

plans had to be top secret. Zack's leaving may have been the tipping point, but nothing was ever disclosed to him or put in writing. Every little detail had to be perfectly planned and stored in her mind. It was imperative no evidenced linked her to the acts. She established a regimented routine; created a systematic approach. Revenge returned a zest for life, and she felt more alive than she had in years – almost giddy with it.

Now life held excitement. She had a reason to wake. Momentum was vital. Each morning she would rise at five, stroll into the kitchen and flick on the kettle then make her way to the shower. Daniel's words of concern resonated but nothing could discourage her. After all, this was her journey. Propelling her enthusiasm forward she created a chant.

"I am strong. Each day I get stronger. They are weak. They will pay." She would sing this in the shower – over and over as the soap suds and warm water cleansed her body and washed away any doubt. Each day the positive effects of her actions strengthened. Her coffee was an essential part of her routine. Her requirement to leave her house by 6:30am became easier as the days passed. Opening her front door to the world no longer held fear but was a feat of bravery. Her confidence grew. She knew ease and comfort would eventually follow. It was all up to her, she controlled her own destiny. Her courage would set her free.

Leaving her house she welcomed the world back into her life. She would drive, park, wait, and watch. Watching and patience were extremely important. Bridget was not the only one who had a regimented routine. Hunters never just rushed in. They possessed patience. The element of surprise was essential, otherwise the prey would be spooked and would escape. Her observations were crucial. Escape would not be an option. Now she began her quest there was no turning back. A half job was no job at all. It was a moment of great clarity. Bridget was committed.

Samuel Easton would be the first.

He had taken great delight in watching her humiliation. The enthusiasm with which he embarked on acts that would result in great embarrassment for Bridget was unrelenting. She had tried to reason with him – he was a married man with a teenage daughter, surely he of all people would understand and relate to the damage inflicted. How would he like to see his wife or daughter subject to such artful acts?

Her begging still haunted her. *'Please Samuel I am asking you, please leave me alone… think about your wife or daughter, what if they received this type of treatment? Surely you wouldn't like it happening to them. I've done nothing to deserve this.'*

How weak she had sounded. He hadn't listened to her pleas; he'd laughed in her face. Told her she was pathetic. He'd insisted she hadn't deserved the job, and declared it took a man to run the show, not a weak, snivelling female.

He'd sneered at her when he'd yelled she should find another job, that she wasn't welcome there. He'd threatened that he'd only just begun. *'Watch your step,'* he'd spat, *'Arthur has you in his sights, as does Pierre.'*

Samuel Easton, Arthur Fuller, and Pierre Rainer had been mates for years. They ran in a pack, and were going to make her life a living hell. He'd been right. He'd run back to Pierre and Arthur and boasted of how he'd made her quiver and cry.

The ferocity of his attacks increased. He stuck labels on the back of her chair at work with 'we are watching you' and 'everyone hates you.' She found funeral notices with her name on them in her desk drawer. He wrote 'whore' and 'slut' in the dirt and dust that appeared on her car. Laughed and scoffed when she walked past. Paranoia kicked in when she saw him whispering to other members of staff who would laugh as she walked by. He placed obscene and nasty drawings depicting her as a stick figure on the workplace notice board. Her name scrawled above the figure with oversized tits, down on hands and knees, being fucked by a dog. Everyone laughed. Samuel even hacked her work e-mail and changed her position title from Manager to maggot – anything to instil humiliation and embarrassment. It was mental torture. Paranoia was her constant companion. His punishment would befit his crimes. Samuel Easton would be seen for the prick he was.

Sitting in her car she watched and waited. A wig, cap and sunglasses aided in her disguise. No one would recognise her car. No one would pay attention to a woman who appeared to be talking on a mobile phone, in a new model Ford sitting two doors down on the opposite side of the road from Samuel Easton's house.

CHAPTER FOUR

The first glimpse of the morning sun peeked out from behind the clouds. New light revealed colour and life. The air was cool. All was still. All was quiet. A single light shone from inside Samuel's brick Californian bungalow. His well-maintained and solid-looking house was set back from the roadway. It was a weekday, and he would soon leave for work. His wife would follow shortly after with their daughter. Pulling back the sleeve to her large jacket, Bridget glanced at her watch. Her attack was rapidly approaching. Nerves began to flutter in her stomach. Fear she would be caught began to create doubt. The steering wheel was slick beneath her sweaty hands. Perspiration trickled from beneath her arms. Bridget glanced over her shoulder checking that everything she required was safely stashed behind the passenger seat. It was. She was prepared. The windows in her car began to fog up, so she cracked her driver's-side window and focused on his house. Waiting.

A group of exercise junkies ran past, their chatter loud and startling. It launched her into a painful memory. She was back at Wolf Industries...

She'd just arrived at work and was sitting at her desk when the telephone rang. She attempted to answer it, not knowing the handset had been stuck to the receiver. The telephone smacked her in the face. Her right cheekbone began to throb.

Laughter erupted. She dropped the telephone. Tears welled in her eyes and she grabbed for a tissue. Pulling hard she got more than she bargained for. She screamed. Attached to the tissue was a large hairy spider. It all happened so quickly that she hadn't the time to realise it was plastic. She burst into tears and ran from her office. Echoes of laughter erupted, followed her as she fled to seclusion of the bathroom. Her cheek was bruised and pulsating. She was embarrassed, upset, and humiliated. Fearful as to what would happen next, she hid in a cubicle.

A door slammed, just as it did when she was hidden away in the cubicle. This time it came from outside her car and she was propelled to the present. Tears lingered in her eyes. Her determination for payback returned. Samuel Easton would not get away with what he'd done.

The image of people standing around her desk pointing fingers and laughing at her played on repeat in her mind. She needed to cast those thoughts aside and remain focused. As the runners disappeared over the hill all became quiet.

She watched.

She waited.

Movement.

Finally, there was movement. Samuel opened the front door. Bridget slunk down in the driver's seat. She peered over the steering wheel. Nausea swirled in her gut. She stared as he threw his lunch bag over his shoulder and strolled to the familiar red, beaten-up Volkswagen that sat in his driveway. He'd purchased it years ago; it was his pride and joy. It appeared nothing much had changed for Samuel Easton, and the feelings she held towards him hadn't changed either.

Watching him made her sick to the stomach. He appeared so smug. If she were a man, she would have wiped that smile off his face years ago. Bridget's anger grew as she watched him climb into his car. Her jaw tensed, she glared. Gripping the steering wheel she maintained her focus. Patience would be her virtue.

Samuel's car roared to life, backfired, released a puff of smoke and in no time he was speeding down the road and over the hill. So far everything was going to plan.

Five minutes passed. Then five more. The front door opened. This time it was his wife. But something was wrong – she was running early. She never ran early. Normally, she wouldn't leave until eight thirty. Watching her dash towards her car, Bridget realised she had another major issue – Samuel's daughter was missing. Where the bloody hell was his daughter? Without everyone accounted for, her mission would be impossible.

"Fuck!" she exclaimed. "Fuck! Fuck! Fuck!"

Sitting still Bridget contemplated her next move. She watched as the car disappeared from sight then recalled Daniel's words: *"Your past may shape your future but your mind determines your actions."*

Was she crazy to believe her strategy would deliver peace? She closed her eyes and wondered if she would be better off abandoning her plan. But if she did, wouldn't she be giving in? Wouldn't that mean she was nothing more than a failure? Time passed. Bridget remained put. Hearing a car approach she ducked her head. It was a silver Mitsubishi station wagon. It was Veronica, Samuel's wife. Bridget silently cheered. Hope returned. Thoughts of abandoning her mission vanished. Her patience returned as Veronica leapt from her car and dashed into the house. The waiting game recommenced.

Minutes passed with no sound or movement. The front door to Samuel's house was finally thrust open. Out emerged his wife Veronica and their daughter Sharon, voices raised. Sharon was complaining about her dad while her mother attempted to quell her grievances by justifying her husband's actions.

"He is a busy man, like your father says… us women will

never understand the pressure a man endures. It is our duty as the females in the family to look after him. He needs his space. It's not too much for him to expect the house to be tidy and for his meals to be served on time. You know what time he leaves for work – every day is the same time. I do not understand why you would interrupt his routine by using the bathroom when you know it is going to annoy him."

"Annoy him? What about me?" Sharon cried.

"You… you should learn to wait, just as I wait. You'll see, one day young lady you will be married and you will understand the importance of keeping your husband happy."

"Married," she huffed. "If this is what it's like when you get married then I am never going to marry. Oh no, I take that back. I'm going to become a lesbian, at least women know how to treat each other with respect."

"Sharon Easton, you watch your tongue," Veronica snapped. "If your father heard you say that you wouldn't have a tongue left in your head! Not another word, I will not listen to another word!"

Both car doors slammed. The loud bang of metal against metal with only a thin strip of rubber seal between plus the revving of the car engine illustrated the frustration of the Easton women. Bridget continued to hear raised voices as Veronica reversed out of the driveway. She couldn't help but smile. It appeared she was not the only one with grievances towards Samuel Easton. She wondered how his daughter would react to her plan.

The time for action was fast approaching. Bridget reached over towards the passenger seat as if retrieving something as Veronica reversed back within meters from her car. Her heart thumped so fast she felt as though it would burst. She swallowed hard. Veronica's car stood next to Bridget before she placed it into drive and took off down the road.

The sound of raised voices and the car soon faded into stillness. Bridget breathed a sigh of relief. Sitting back up, she scanned the street. All was silent but she waited. Waited for enough time to pass so it would reduce the chance of being caught. Normally they wouldn't return until the afternoon, but there was always a small chance something could have been forgotten. It was better to be safe than sorry.

Ten minutes passed. With the house vacant and no activity within the street Bridget climbed out of her car. She scanned the street, ears pricked. Her heart pounded. She wiped her sweaty palms down her jacket. There was no turning back.

Moving around to the passenger side she opened the back door and retrieved all she required. Weapon clenched in her right hand, another quick scan ensured the coast was still clear. She dashed across the road.

Inside the gate and on the front lawn, she froze. Doubt crept in. She crouched struggling to maintain composure, and remained still until she could catch her breath. The thought of the arrogance she witnessed in Samuel's eyes soon evaporated her hesitation and fear. His arrogance would soon be wiped from his face and be replaced with humiliation and embarrassment.

Rising to her feet she took another moment to compose herself. She inhaled deeply and reminded herself who started it. She wouldn't be there had they not treated her so badly, so cruelly. *I'll show everyone what you are.*

She sucked in the cool morning air, placed her white face mask over her nose and mouth, securing the elastic strap over her ears and behind her head. She walked swiftly from behind the front fence towards his house. A straight line. Her focus was on a brick line at the front wall of his house. She paused, turned to her right then circled the massive lawn – it had to be at least fifteen meters wide and possibly ten meters deep with only a driveway to the left of the block. She returned to the front fence and again walked directly towards his house. Speed and attention to detail were her friends; she needed to be smart.

The next few minutes were spent focusing on her steps and dwelling over the pain Samuel had inflicted. His lawn was another pride and joy. His lush, well-manicured buffalo lawn would be her canvas. She continually scanned the street. There was no sign of life. Bridget was alone. She would soon be on her way. Her job would be complete. Before she knew it, she was striding the last path towards his house. The anticipation of her results made her smile. The outcome would begin to show in a matter of days.

Dashing across the road she opened the rear door and threw in her tools. She slammed the door closed and jumped into the driver's seat. Removing her mask, she flung it onto the back seat.

"Woohoo!"

It was a moment of great jubilation. Tears of overwhelming joy streamed down her face. *What a rush!* She was pumped. She was done. She felt invigorated. Alive.

Driving home, she knew she just needed to wait. So she did. She carried on with her daily routine as she thought about her next move. She had another visit from Zack and she spoke with Daniel on the telephone – assured him she was fine.

She waited patiently. Drive-by events occurred every morning. Nearly a week had passed before she began to spot glimpses of yellow. Yellow changed to brown. Blades of grass began to wither and die. The affected area grew. Prominent lines and curves formed.

Three weeks later her masterpiece appeared. It was a stroke of genius. Samuel Easton was a prick and his lawn announced his presence in bold, eight-meter high capitals.

He was mortified.

Bridget drank a toast to her successful mission.

Revenge was sweet. The negative feelings associated with Samuel Easton would no longer evoke fear or anxiety. A sense of power returned. Samuel Easton was just the start. Her job was incomplete. It was her duty as a responsible citizen to report an act of vandalism. She made an anonymous report to the local newspaper. The good people in her neighbourhood deserved to know what was happening.

The newspaper jumped on the story. Her masterpiece was photographed. A photo of Samuel Easton and his vandalised lawn ended up as front-page news. He was quoted: 'I am outraged! To think someone would take delight in attacking another person, it's disgusting.' The newspaper publicised his address, which resulted in further humiliation and embarrassment. Traffic flow in his street increased tenfold. People stood out the front taking photos, laughing and pointing. Samuel was forced to submit an application for leave. He spent the few next weeks as a recluse, hidden away from prying eyes.

The world would forever link Samuel Easton to the word 'PRICK'. Social media went into meltdown:

What's another name for prick? Samuel Easton.

What's eight meters high and thirteen meters wide? Samuel Easton's new name tag.

Who should have gone to Spec Savers before using weed killer? Samuel Easton.

Who's a prick? You're a prick! No I'm not – Samuel Easton is a prick.

P.R.I.C.K what does it spell? Samuel Easton.

It was like sitting back and watching a circus. Samuel had been made to look more than just a clown. Bridget wondered if his feelings of embarrassment and humiliation compared to the way he had made her feel. She had no regrets. Had his payback been sufficient?

Oh, she was just getting started.

CHAPTER FIVE

Bridget knew what she wanted as she cast her eyes over Daniel. She wanted the good doctor. Her thoughts went well beyond talking. With Zack out of the picture there was no reason why she couldn't pursue another man. Things that had never crossed her mind were surfacing. Suppressed thoughts and feelings. She felt like a wild animal released from its cage. Like a lioness on the prowl. Revitalised, energised. Ready to strike. She was liberated. Daniel was single. She was single. He said he enjoyed her company. She knew she enjoyed his. Why couldn't they take their relationship to another level? But what if she told him how she felt and her feelings were not reciprocated? Voicing how she felt could drive a wedge into their relationship. Opening her mouth prematurely could destroy what they shared. Just because he said he enjoyed her company didn't mean he wanted more. Friends enjoyed the company of friends. Sitting in the familiar corner of his room, she closed her eyes and contemplated her next move. *Why wouldn't you? Don't pass up the opportunity. You only live once.*

"Bridget… are you okay?" Daniel asked.

Her eyes sprung open. "Yes, I was just thinking about my feelings," she said with a sniff.

Staring across the room she locked onto his eyes. They were gorgeous, so kind and caring and his lips were so pink and soft looking. She wanted to taste his breath, wanted to feel his body next to hers, wanted to place her hands, her mouth all over his body. She crossed her legs, closed her eyes and bit her lip. She imagined. She released an elongated sigh. Tears welled in her eyes. She didn't want to lose him. His rejection would be devastating. For now she would remain silent. She would talk about what she knew best.

"Have you ever feared someone or something so much that the thought of them or it makes you physically ill? You have to force yourself not to think, but distraction is impossible," she said. "Fear infiltrates your every move. Wrapped tightly around your body you begin to feel suffocated. You're slowly dying as the fear consumes. Sucking away life. You remain a shell of your former self. Trapped within indestructible barriers. Barriers once created to protect now destroy as darkness overshadows your every move." She clenched her hands as she spoke. "Despair invades, and finally you wake up one morning thinking, why me? Surely this isn't the life I was expected to have. You wonder why bother. Then comes the hatred."

She leant forward in her seat, eyes locked to his. "Have you ever experienced hatred so much that it feels like it bubbles up from inside? Your mind wishes you could strike down those you despise. A vile putrid taste dances within your mouth. Your body pulsates, anger stirs and you walk around as if balancing on a hair trigger. One wrong move and things could explode," she said, and he didn't look away. "Issues twist into existence, feeding frustration and igniting anger. Your life spins out of control until finally it feels a bit like going down a long dark alley with no torch and no end of darkness in sight. We live in a world full of dangers, Daniel. Bullies, perpetrators of violent acts and killers exist; they mingle amongst us unnoticed. They strike and disappear into the night until they strike again. The odds are on their side. Unsuspecting victims are left with emotional and sometimes physical scars. How many of them are actually out there? How many will ever be caught and punished? There's a monster in all of us, if given the chance to be born."

Daniel remained silent as she spoke. So many variations of the same he had heard – fear, anger, hate, sadness, thoughts of revenge. He wanted to wrap his arms around her, comfort her and take away her pain. Since their first meeting he had admired her, and his feelings had grown stronger over time. Now with Zack gone there was no reason he should hold his tongue. He was single. She was single. She'd said she enjoyed talking with him. Why not take their relationship to another level? But would he be overstepping the mark? She was his patient. What if she felt he had taken advantage of her? Voicing how he felt about her could destroy their relationship. But if he did it respectfully, so as not to offend or embarrass then surely she would understand, and they would remain friends. She had to know his primary concern was her welfare.

"Bridget, I want to ask you a question."

He paused, and she looked up from the other side of the room. Her head tilted to the side and her brows furrowed.

"What? You can ask me anything, Daniel."

"I have been thinking about you a lot lately. I don't want you to take what I am about to say the wrong way," he said and gave her a short smile. "You must know I care about you a great deal. I want what is in your best interests."

Bridget leant forward in her chair, staring directly into his eyes, her attention fully focussed on him.

"Bridget…" he hesitated, unsure how to proceed.

"Yes, Daniel?"

"I want you to be honest with me."

"I *am* honest with you, Daniel."

Daniel rose from his chair and walked around to the front of his desk. Bridget's gaze never strayed from him. He stopped and lent back against his desk, his eyes locked to hers.

"Was it you?" he asked.

"Sorry?"

"Did you poison Samuel Easton's lawn?"

Bridget turned bright red, answering his questions before she spoke it.

"Yes," she replied.

Daniel shook his head, kept his face composed as he watched her. She gulped nervously, but her eyes never left his. Finally, he smiled then clapped.

"Bravo," he chuckled. "Bravo, bravo, bravo."

Tears welled in Bridget's eyes, and she swallowed hard. Her body twitched, almost as if she was going to leap into his arms. But that was wishful thinking, so he schooled a serious stare before he spoke again. "I congratulate you, but I must also warn you. Your acts of revenge may end in pain, and I worry you will be caught. Where will it end? What happens if they discover you were behind this?"

A brief flash of pain appeared in her eyes before she shut it down. "If I do nothing they won't pay."

"They *will* pay. We all pay for our actions. Tell me what happens if they recognise you?"

"They won't," she said. "I wore a large coat, oversized combat boots. I bound my chest so I didn't even look like a female. I wore shoulder pads and a face mask. I also have a balaclava just in case, and I know how I can distort my voice."

Daniel sat staring, amazed at the amount of thought she had put into her revenge but fearful her actions would be exposed. As her treating psychiatrist he could make suggestions and recommendations but he could not control her actions.

"Please think long and hard before you do anything else," he begged.

Bridget nodded. "I will."

The timer buzzed; her therapy session had expired. Bridget rose from her chair and Daniel from the desk. They stood face to face.

"Bridget, before you leave can I say one more thing?" He gave her a small smile when she nodded. "You walk around with clenched fists, you hold to your anger but at some stage you have to let go. You have to open your arms to what lies before you. You have to be grateful for what you have. It's not about focusing on your suffering and loss, and it's not about the have nots in life, it is about the haves. What you have now and what you have to look forward to. Please think about what you have in your life."

Bridget nodded but remained silent as she studied his face. His words were genuine. She felt so comfortable with him, so at ease. He didn't make her feel lesser even though she knew he was highly educated and extremely intelligent. Zack was just over six feet tall, but his demeanour had left her feeling like he looked down on her, as if she was inferior. With Daniel, she could look him in the eyes – they were equally matched. It was almost as if they were made for each other.

People said everything happened for a reason. Maybe she had to go through her trauma so she would meet him – a dark experience that had a bright and beautiful future ahead. Under normal circumstances she probably wouldn't mix with a psychiatrist; they'd have run in different circles. Maybe Daniel was right. Maybe he was her pot of gold at the end of a rainbow. She'd survived a stormy experience, had released a deluge of tears. If he was her pot of gold then the rainbow may have represented the colourful path she had to travel after the storm of Wolf Industries.

Bridget blinked rapidly, trying to fight away her tears. She wanted to hug him but didn't want to ruin what they shared.

"I will, Daniel. I'll try, thank you."

CHAPTER SIX

Bridget took a deep breath and for a moment stared into space. Peeking out the window she watched. If she had learnt anything over the past years, it was patience. Beyond her half-opened blinds grey clouds massed. A storm was brewing.

Wolf Industries and the people who'd tried to destroy her, dominated her thoughts. Distraction was only temporary. She wondered about the effects of a lobotomy. If this procedure were still available today would she seek out a surgeon? She knew it seemed drastic. To have an orbitoclast stuck in behind your eye, to tear apart connections in your brain. But how else could she rid herself of the horrid thoughts and feelings? She wanted them gone. She *needed* them gone. *Am I going crazy?*

Peace. She needed peace and calm. She burst into tears. Screamed until her throat hurt. She clenched her hands then punched the bed beside her again and again and again. Her head began to pound and she collapsed on the bed. *I hate popping pills.* Medication had side effects. She had piled on the weight, and felt like a big mass of blubber.

"Fuck! Fuck! Fuck!" She hated them. If she had a baseball bat and they were standing in front of her right now, she would bring them to their knees. She would make them feel pain like she had felt pain. Scar them for the rest of their lives she would. And as they hobbled around in pain, they would remember the pain they'd inflicted with every step they took. They would never forget. Nor should they. If she couldn't forget, why should they?

Samuel Easton had been her warm up. One down, three to go.

Next on her list was Arthur Fuller. Arthur had a big mouth and had been only too happy to spread lies and rumours. He was a gossip monger who loved to embellish stories and didn't care about the ramifications of his actions. His behaviour was anything but normal for a mature-aged man. His words destroyed self-confidence.

Arthur would soon know what it felt like to be on the receiving end. He would feel the crippling effect; his life restricted. Required to defend his actions, he would be overwhelmed with anxiety. Fear of potential danger would haunt him. Uneasiness would create stress. Gossip would destroy. He would learn that anxiety was a handicap. Invisible to the eye, nonetheless it would make completing the most basic of daily tasks a near impossibility. It was a given. All recipients would endure pain. Her prey would bear restrictions for the remainder of his life.

Arthur had been married to his devoted wife Jill for thirty-two years. She was a trusting soul who had walked around with her head in the sand, oblivious to his lewd and cheating behaviour. It was time for her to receive a little enlightenment. His blatant lack of respect for his wife and the female population would be exposed. Fingers crossed if her plan worked, his infidelity would cost him. You see it was Jill who held the purse strings in their relationship. Arthur had married into a family of great wealth, had spruiked how she liked to keep him happy. What Arthur wanted, Arthur got. Face to face, he would display love and affection – the devoted and caring husband. Behind her back, he referred to her as a 'cow'. Calling her as ugly as a hat full of arseholes and a crap root. Surely, she would not tolerate a lying, cheating bastard.

Hell hath no fury like a woman scorned. Her humiliation and embarrassment would be replaced by strength. Freedom would be bestowed upon her as she reclaimed her vitality. Fuck-around Arthur would be fucked to the gutter where he belonged.

Watching him became a sport, a challenge. Samuel Easton had been her introduction to the art of revenge. Momentum increased. Plans excited. Bravery and self-confidence evolved. Each possessed their individual traits, certain routines and rituals. Arthur always checked his mailbox before leaving in the morning and as soon as he returned at night. It was a puzzling action. The postman only delivered during the day. It was almost as if he were waiting for something. That would be his weakness. Intercept his mail. Ruin his marriage.

Arthur Fuller had made Bridget the butt of all jokes. She would make him feel more than embarrassment. Just his name brought painful memories, and she was back at Wolf Industries…

She had been walking towards the kitchen area when she heard echoes of laughter. *Someone must be telling a joke,* she thought, *after my morning from hell I wouldn't mind having a good laugh.*

She smiled as she entered the kitchen. "Hey what's so funny?"

The room turned deadly silent. Arthur Fuller, head of Accounts Payable quickly yanked a piece of paper from the bench trying to conceal it behind his back. His face was aglow. No one said a word. Guilty shades of ghostly white and flushing crimson red coloured their faces. Stepping forward with hands on his hips Pierre remarked smugly, "It's a private joke, nothing to do with you. Anyway, we were just leaving its starting to smell like crap in here. I think you should get the sewer looked at, the smell of shit appears everywhere I go today."

Like a herd of sheep they followed him out of the room, faces to the floor. No one dared look Bridget in the eye.

The feeling of isolation and rejection was like a slap in the face. Bridget was supposed to be a part of a team. They were supposed to work together. Yet, their actions made her feel as though she was a transplanted organ, incompatible with the main body. Attacked at every opportunity with no remedy in sight. Tears began to well in her eyes. She couldn't understand why she was being treated this way. Why were her complaints to senior management being ignored? She was performing well in her job; the turn-around in business performance and the positive effects on the bottom line spoke for themselves. Wolf Industries was making more money than it had for a long time. Yet, she endured rudeness and smug remarks daily.

Taking a deep breath she was determined they would never see how their antics affected her. She was stronger than they thought, and wouldn't crumble beneath their bullying behaviour. A nice cup of tea would settle her upset. The kettle boiled and her teabag released the strong brew. Turning her attention to the notice board she was floored, sickened.

"What the heck!"

Bridget snatched the paper from the board. Glancing around, she couldn't see another soul. She was alone. *How dare they!* The bitter taste of bile rose to her throat at the violation. Her pulse throbbed in her forehead. She knew exactly who was responsible but had no proof. In her hand was a picture of a naked, obese woman. A cut-out photo of her face had been stuck upon the large double chin. Rolls upon rolls of marshmallow skin cascaded over the body. Pimple-like nipples dripped from engorged breasts. Dimpled arms, and with legs the size of tree trunks spread wide open. They had been laughing at *her*. Again. They wanted her to bite, to crumble, to cave but she wouldn't give them the satisfaction. Complaining to management would see her labelled as trivial, a trouble-maker. It was obvious from previous management responses that they were not taking her seriously.

Remaining silent and seemingly unaffected was the better option. *Rise above it. Walk out with your head held high.*

CHAPTER SEVEN

A rthur Fuller was a lying, cheating creature. Bridget was compelled to be a facilitator of the truth. For the truth would set him more than just free. Honesty and gossip would expose and destroy him. Bridget's plan would strip him in more ways than one. Her elaborate scheme was set out in three stages. His wife deserved to know the all. Arthur would suffer as she had suffered. He would learn the power of lies and gossip. Once words were spoken, they could never be taken back. They would never be forgotten. The damage would be done. But her intent went beyond words. Social media was a delightful tool. Gossip could spread to places far and wide with the velocity of a speeding arrow. Sharp tongues would spread the word.

Over recent weeks, Bridget had embarked upon a series of telephone hang-ups. She would drive to the local telephone box, dial Arthur's home number and when Jill answered she would simply hang up.

As the time got closer for phase two of the operation, doubts began to surface, but she reassured herself of her plan. For it to be a success she would have to rely on Arthur's wife, Jill. It was *her* reaction that would seal Arthur's fate.

Friday was the day. Arthur Fuller, Samuel Easton and Pierre Rainer went to the local pub every Friday night. Bridget had gathered her evidence. She had watched and waited. It was the previous Monday when she had sent an anonymous letter to Jill's workplace. Sending it there meant there was no chance Arthur could intercept it. It was a simple letter with a subtle clue.

The wrongful actions of a man should not result in the ongoing pain experienced by a woman.

The letter was delivered Tuesday afternoon. Bridget had been sitting in the shoe department trying on shoes when Jill was handed the envelope. The shoe department was close enough so she would see and hear everything without being noticed. The mail was delivered at the same time daily. Observing routines and behaviours was crucial. Tearing the envelope open Jill unfolded the piece of paper. Her eyes scanned the page. She looked up, scanning the store then looked down at the page again. Her eyebrows furrowed. Her lips twitched. She raised her left hand to her mouth and bit her nail. Another sales assistant, Julie approached.

"Is everything okay?" Julie asked.

"I'm not sure…look at this," she replied, passing the note to Julie while she inspected the envelope, flipping it from the front to the back. The envelope offered no clues, only Jill's name, and the name of the department store with the address.

"How strange. What does it mean?" Julie asked.

"I'm not sure, but something doesn't feel right. Like something's wrong but you just don't know what. I've been feeling that way for a couple of weeks."

An old lady pushing a shopping trolley approached the counter where they stood. Jill placed the letter back into the envelope and stashed it in the counter drawer. Bridget returned the shoes to the shelf and left the store wondering.

Phase three of her plan would be completed on Friday. It had to be completed. She needed to put Jill out of her misery.

***

Tuesday night Bridget drove to the local telephone box and made the call.

A woman answered. "Good evening, Fuller residence. Jill Fuller speaking."

"Hello, may I speak to Arthur," Bridget replied, in a smooth and sultry voice.

"May I ask who's calling?"

"A friend."

"One moment please."

Bridget listened as Jill summoned Arthur to the phone. He asked who was on the line.

"I don't know. Some strange woman…a friend," Jill said.

"Hello… Hello…" Arthur said. "There's no one there."

Bridget hung up then drove home satisfied with her work. She knew only too well how a person's world begins to collapse as doubt creeps in. Arthur Fuller had taught her that lesson well.

But she couldn't keep Jill hanging. When she ventured into the department store on Wednesday, Jill no longer possessed a happy, smiling face. Her eyes appeared dull and full of suspicion, flicking incessantly around the store. Shame welled in Bridget for inflicting pain upon an innocent woman, but she had no other choice. Arthur had shown no regard for Bridget's personal life, or how his actions would impact her relationship with Zack. She, too, had been an innocent victim.

Before all the issues at Wolf Industries, Bridget had been forgiving, reasonable, and rational. Hurt and survival instincts forced change upon her. Jill Fuller would be collateral damage, but the woman would recover. Arthur Fuller was responsible for the pain his devoted wife experienced. Emotions had to be separated from business. Remaining at a safe distance Bridget would load the gun, but it would be Jill who would fire the bullets. Bridget would watch destruction unfold from afar.

***

Friday afternoon a package was delivered to Jill at work. It contained date-stamped photos from the previous Saturday.

Jill had been at work. The day had been sunny. Arthur had been disappointed at her inability to attend a work function. Jill had purchased him an expensive suit so he would look strikingly professional. But the photos did not show a work gathering at The Hilton where Arthur had claimed he was going. The photos contained only two individuals Jill recognised – Samuel Easton and Pierre Rainer. Jill put a hand to her stomach as Bridget sat in the shoe department, trying on shoes as she watched it all unfold.

The top photo was of Arthur standing proud in his new suit, and appeared to have been taken at a park. Jill smiled. It was obvious she loved Arthur. Bridget had done her homework on the two. They were young when they'd first met, and from all Bridget had gleaned, for Jill, it had been love at first sight. The two had dated for less than a year before Arthur popped the question. Jill had been clearly ecstatic, and Bridget had overheard the woman telling Julie that she'd always viewed herself as the ugly duckling, but Arthur had said she was his rainbow, that she added colour to a world that at times appeared dull.

They were married on their first anniversary.

Flick.

Jill placed the first photo to the back of the pile. Her smile was quickly replaced by a look of shock and horror. Same park. Same pond in the background. This time Arthur was not alone. No doubt she wondered who the strange person was. No doubt she wondered where the photo had been taken. And who had taken the photo?

Flick.

Tears welled in Jill's eyes as she studied the next photo. Her face reddened, and she quickly looked up and scanned the store to see if anyone was watching. Bridget ducked her head and reached for another pair of shoes. Jill's hands began to shake. She shook her head.

Flick.

Jill's eyebrows furrowed. Her face reddened. Her knees weakened. She sat on the chair behind her counter. She continued to shake her head. Bridget began to feel her pain. She knew things would only get worse. She was relieved. The counter was glass. Her view was not obstructed. She felt compelled to watch.

Flick.

Tears streamed down Jill's face. With each photo she became more distressed. Julie moved to Jill's side. Bridget knew the order of the photos. Jill was looking at the one of Arthur with his arm around a young woman's waist. Julie placed her hand on Jill's shoulder, attempting to comfort the woman. Jill's shaking continued, as did her viewing of the photos.

Flick.

Next, Arthur danced with the same young woman. Jill placed her hand over her mouth. Her shaking continued. Her jaw clenched. Her face was aglow. Tears ran down her cheeks.

Flick.

Next, Samuel Easton and his wife, Pierre Rainer and his partner, along with Arthur and this unknown younger woman posed for photos together. Jill's eyes widened. Now she knew her husband had lied to her. Bridget could see in Jill's face the connections finally coming together. The mysterious phone calls. The strange letter. And now the evidence that spoke for itself. It looked as if her husband was having an affair. The unknown woman looked Asian in appearance and was about the same age as their daughter – who was in her twenties. Bridget watched as Jill put her hand to her mouth, as if she felt sick. Betrayal did that. She had been sleeping with a man who could have brought home any disease, and with what Jill now held in her hand, he would not be able to talk himself out of this one.

Flick.

A new photo revealed Arthur all over the younger woman. His hands touching places no hand should travel in public. Jill began huffing and puffing. Her face contorted. Her nostrils flared. She was furious.

Flick.

Devastation hit. Shock. Horror. Anger. Despair. They all took a turn on Jill's face. Bridget watched, somewhat shamefully, as Jill began heaving. The woman swallowed hard, and clutched at her chest. Her breath appeared restricted. Bridget could well guess what Jill was thinking: how could she have been so gullible, so trusting? How long had it been going on? The man she loved was a liar.

From across the department store Bridget watched as the photos fell to the floor. Jill Fuller burst into tears. Her bellowing cries became an instant siren for all eyes. Her pain witnessed by many. Bridget heard the whispers that theorised the assistant might have just been informed of a death. Why else would a woman burst into hysterics? But Bridget knew the truth. Arthur Fuller would not be able to deny his actions. The final photo had been a hotel room receipt with his signature dated last Saturday. Jill had been working. The name on the receipt was Mr and Mrs Fuller. Champagne. Room service. Meals for two. Adult movie charges. A pamper package for two.

Julie crouched and tried to console Jill, but it was clear Jill was crushed, too distraught. Tears ran like rivers down her cheeks and drenched her white blouse. Five minutes passed before her cries began to subside.

Bridget watched on, saddened by the pain. *With every action, there has to be a reaction and a consequence, endings require beginnings. Arthur Fuller was the instigator.* Jill slowly gathered her emotions and wiped away her tears. Her cheeks were flushed. Her eyes were red and puffy. She pushed to her feet with the assistance of Julie. Her sniffling echoed around the store as she shuffled from behind the counter. Head down, Bridget watched as Jill struggled to hold back more tears.

Jill trudged out the front door and to her car. Bridget followed. Maintaining her distance, she parked up the street, on the opposite side of the road.

In two hours Arthur would be home.

CHAPTER EIGHT

Sitting behind her steering wheel, Bridget kept an eye on the time. All had been quiet in the Fuller house. Arthur would soon come speeding up the road in his black Audi sports car. Bridget's anticipation of what would unfold had resulted in her feeling both nauseated and excited. She shivered. The hairs on her arms stood to attention. Her brow was lathered in sweat. Her hands were so clammy she had to continually wipe them dry. Before she had a chance to think about anything else, she spotted Arthur's car.

Sliding down behind the steering wheel she peeked out the drivers' window and watched as Arthur climbed from his car. His routine never changed. He checked his letterbox then proceeded to his front door. The sight of him made her sick to the stomach. He strutted to the door like a proud chicken. She could only hope he would soon be plucked. Leaping the stairs he stuck his key in the front door and before she knew it he had disappeared inside.

Bridget sat still. She watched. She listened. She waited for the explosion. Time passed. All was quiet. She began to worry her plan had failed, and feared his wife might have been the forgiving type – weak and accepting of her husband's indiscretions. This was not the response she'd expected. Half an hour went by. All remained silent. She wondered what was happening behind the closed doors. Venturing closer risked being seen. Leaving now could result in her missing the fireworks. She had to remain where she was. Another thirty minutes passed. A taxi pulled into the Fuller driveway and beeped its horn. Arthur dashed out the door, slamming it behind him. He jumped into the taxi. The taxi drove up the street and out of sight.

Bridget was dumbfounded. She'd heard no yelling. Maybe his wife had shown him the evidence and he had killed her in a fit of rage. Maybe she was dead. How was it he could dash down to a taxi and jump in as if he hadn't a care in the world? Bridget knew exactly where he was going. Within minutes he would be at the pub drinking with his mates, Samuel Easton and Pierre Rainer. It was time to leave. Her mission had failed. She felt sick to the stomach. Defeated. Arthur Fuller had won. She needed to reassess her plans.

Placing her key into the ignition Bridget started her car. Looking over her shoulder she checked to make sure all was clear before she drove away. Arthur Fuller's street was much busier than Samuel Easton's. A yellow car approached from behind and so she waited. Glancing back towards Arthur's house hope returned. She saw movement. The garage door was opening. Jill Fuller was alive.

Bridget sighed in relief and pulled up to the kerb. Switching off the ignition, she watched and waited until Jill Fuller exited the garage with a large pile of clothes and dumped them in the centre of her front lawn before disappearing around the side of the house. Moments later she returned with a garden hose, which she dropped next to the pile of clothes. A quick trip to the garage, and Jill returned with a green petrol can.

Bridget smiled. Her heart began to race as she clenched her steering wheel and silently cheered Jill on. This was a woman on a mission. The power behind Jill's strides illustrated her determination. Opening the can Jill emptied its contents over the clothes. She lit a match. Dropped it onto the pile. Flames leapt, and she jumped back and grabbed the hose. Passing cars slowed to see what was happening. Jill Fuller waved them on, her face lit with smiles of delight.

Within a couple of minutes all that remained was a pile of flickering embers and ashes. Jill Fuller doused the embers and cheered. She fist-punched the air and Bridget cheered along with her. She felt like dashing over and hugging the woman, but knew that was impossible.

Jill Fuller returned into the garage with a spring in her step. Seconds later, she returned and this time she was carrying a large paint tin and paint brush. She plonked it down next to Arthur's car then walked around inspecting all the panels. Returning to the back of the car she ran her fingers over the window. Paused. Finally she dipped the brush into the can, her hand moving quickly to the top left corner of the window as she began to paint…

Arthur,

Jill paused and stepped back to admire her work. Bridget watched on with bated breath. She could only imagine what Jill was going to do next – surely not just his name. Jill approached the car again, dipped her brush into the tin and continued. White paint dripped over the driveway as she worked. Her enthusiasm increased and her brush strokes became vigorous and passionate. By the time she was finished, Bridget wasn't the only person watching. The woman's masterpiece was done. A few people cheered. Others clapped. Jill stood back and took a bow before turning to admire her work.

The whole world would know exactly what she thought. They would know what a lying cheating bastard her husband was.

Arthur,
This car belongs to me. Not to you
and certainly not to your WHORE.
Regards,
Your soon to be ex-wife.

Bridget could not contain her excitement. She roared with laughter. She clapped her hands as tears ran down her face. She was witnessing a woman who possessed power. Jill collected the paint tin from the drive and with one last rush of determination she tipped the remaining contents over the bonnet. It looked as if a large seagull had flown over and completed its business.

Arthur Fuller wouldn't know what hit him.

CHAPTER NINE

Bridget watched and waited. One hour passed. Darkness enveloped the sky. The night air carried coolness. Stars sparkled overhead. Arthur Fuller would soon be home. The streetlights blinked on. The fireworks would soon begin. Bridget wanted a Bourbon. She felt like a smoke – the kind you had after great sex. But this was better than any sex she'd experienced.

The front door opened, and Jill Fuller stepped onto the verandah. In her hand she held a large board that she placed on the step. Bridget sat upright in her seat, trying to figure out what was going on.

Jill disappeared back into the house, and returned moments later hammer in hand. She began to hammer the large board to the verandah's front post. Bridget couldn't believe her eyes; this woman wanted to be heard. She was no fool. She wouldn't accept Arthur's behaviour. Jill stood back and admired her masterpiece, nodded, then headed inside, slamming the door behind her.

Jill's words sung out loud and clear. Arthur Fuller wouldn't know what hit him.

The suit I purchased for you to wear with
your whore is in that pile of ashes on my lawn.
My car you used to drive is staying here.

What was your home is now my house.
Go screw someone else Arthur Fuller.
You will be hearing from my solicitor.
My pre-nup means you get nothing!

Bridget burst into fits of laughter. Her plan couldn't have worked any better if she'd tried. Without Arthur… So the waiting game continued. Bridget tapped her fingers on the steering wheel; she needed to pee. But she had to stay put. Arthur would soon be home – ten more minutes. It paid to know his routine. She hoped he was enjoying his last beer. Bridget was sure swallowing would be difficult when he arrived home.

Headlights appeared at the end of the street. A taxi approached. She gripped her steering wheel tight, unable to drag her eyes from the vehicle. The taxi continued. *Damn, false alarm.* Surely he wouldn't be far away. Bridget could well imagine him leaving the pub now, he and his buddies laughing. No doubt they would have been scheming and plotting. When they were together they acted as though they were untouchable.

Headlights swung into the street again. Another taxi approached. This time it began to slow as Bridget's heart began to race. The taxi stopped, and the internal light in the taxi flicked on. Bridget watched as Arthur paid for his fare. Watched as he got out of the taxi – oblivious. He staggered up the driveway, and the verandah's front sensor light blinked on. Arthur flinched, took a stumbling step back. He raised his hand to his forehead. Even from her position she could see him pale, turn as white as a ghost. He collapsed to his knees.

"Jill! Please! It was a stupid mistake," he bellowed. "A one-off! I was drunk… Jill! Please!"

The front door remained closed. Arthur began to sob then looked around to see if anyone was watching. He struggled to his feet. Stared up at the sky. He walked over the lawn and kicked at the ashes. From the slump in his shoulders, it was clear he was beginning to understand the gravity of his situation. Jill wasn't coming out. He staggered to his car, but it wouldn't open. He desperately reefed on the door handles as he wailed.

He made his way to the rear of the car.

"No!" he shrieked. "This can't be happening!"

Lights from next door and across the road began to flick on – one after another. People crept outside, staring as Arthur staggered up the front steps and began pounding on his front door.

"Let me in! Jill, let me in," he barked. "I can explain. You don't understand!"

The door remained closed. The verandah light snapped off. No explanation was necessary. No words would suffice.

Arthur collapsed on the front step. His sobbing echoed from the darkness. He was a man defeated. The door would never open for him.

Bridget started her car, and drove off. Satisfied.

CHAPTER TEN

At home Bridget celebrated her latest achievement with a drink, followed by another and another. Before she knew it, she had gulped away half a large bottle of Bourbon. She was drunk. Sitting on her lounge she heard a loud thud at the front door. The repeated banging that followed snapped her into the present. Staggering to her feet, she swayed. Steadying herself on the hallway wall, she let its smooth surface guide her to the front door. *Who the hell is pounding on my door? Holy shit maybe it is Arthur Fuller.*

Fumbling with the lock she finally managed to get it open. She tugged on the door handle so hard the door flew back hitting her in the side of the head.

"Oh it's you," she slurred. So caught up with her plan for Arthur, she had forgotten her arrangements with Zack.

"You're drunk," he spat. "Was it you? Tell me, was it you?"

"Was it me… what? What are you talking about?"

"What am I talking about? I'm talking about the same thing everyone is talking about. Arthur Fuller, his wife has gone crazy. Painted his car. Kicked him out. The poor bastard rolled into the pub hysterical. He said she's lost the plot."

Bridget laughed. "The bastard deserves everything he gets."

"It was you, wasn't it? First Samuel Easton and now Arthur Fuller. Have you lost your mind? You told her didn't you? I know it was you."

"I don't know what you are talking about! Told her what?"

"Don't lie to me Bridget. I'm not stupid. I had my suspicions with Samuel, but now with Arthur it's too big of a coincidence. Tell me Bridget," he demanded, thrusting his finger towards her face.

"Tell you what? They got what they deserved. I'm here. I've been drinking with all my friends. Can't you see I am having a party?" she said. "Remember me? Have you met all my friends?" she hissed, as she turned around and pointed down the hallway. She closed her eyes. Even behind the darkness of her eyelids the room continued to spin. She couldn't bear to look at him. Who did he think he was to come into her house and make accusations?

"Why don't you get your things and just leave me in peace."

But he wouldn't leave. "Sandra said she saw you."

"Saw me when?"

"She saw you spying on them."

"On whom?"

"You know who, stop playing games. She said she saw you spying on Samuel Easton, Arthur Fuller and Pierre Rainer… last Saturday."

"What about last Saturday?" Bridget said as she grabbed for the collar on her top. Things were heating up. The air became thick. She gulped in a large breath of air. Opened her eyes wide and stared at him. Her jaw clenched; he was starting to get on her nerves.

"You know what? I don't care what you think, and I sure as hell don't care what Suckadick believes she saw. Get your things and leave!"

"Bridget—"

"I said get your things and *leave my house*."

Zack shook his head and stormed off down the hallway. Bridget sighed. At last he was out of her face. Holding onto the wall she battled to maintain her emotions. She felt tears. Not only had she forgotten Zack was coming over, she had also been spotted while spying. Stupid mistakes could have dire consequences. The sound of Zack bashing and crashing in the bedroom made her feel sick to the stomach. She remained silent. To speak could result in him staying longer. She wanted him gone. She wanted to be alone.

Zack came thundering up the hallway. His arms were full of large sports bags overflowing with his clothes and shoes. Pushing past her he had one more thing to say. "I'll be back for more another time but I am warning you…" he paused and turned back staring her in the eyes. She could feel his warm breath on her face. "You are going to end up with more trouble than you can handle. If Sandra and I suspect you are behind this, it's not going to take long for the three amigos to work it out."

Bridget slammed the door in his face. She couldn't be bothered to watch him leave. Her life was no longer his concern. Staggering back down to the lounge room, she flopped onto the couch and poured herself another drink. *To hell with them, to hell with them all.* Tonight was her night to celebrate. Tomorrow would be another day. She would worry then.

As the coolness of her bourbon met her lips she inhaled the sweetness. She closed her eyes. Smiled. She thought of Arthur Fuller sobbing in his driveway.

What goes around, comes around.

She opened her eyes and gazed around her peaceful room. At least she had a roof over her head. She grinned and gulped down another mouthful of Bourbon.

Tomorrow was another day.

CHAPTER ELEVEN

Waking with a thumping headache Bridget rolled out of bed and staggered up the hallway. A trail of clothes showed the path she had taken to bed the previous night. Her first stop of the morning would be her bathroom. Gazing into the mirror she studied her reflection. Her glassy eyes were rimmed with smudged black mascara. Streaky tear stains ran down her cheeks. Last night she had endured more haunting nightmares. If only she could have one undisturbed night of rest. Broken sleep only added to her frustration. She retrieved some headache tablets and slowly closed the medicine cabinet. Again, she stood studying her face. What would it take to forget? The mirror offered no answers and so she continued to the kitchen.

She rubbed her eyes, as she struggled to focus on the stove clock. It was just after eight and her therapy with Daniel was at ten. Therapy was always scheduled for the same time. It was easier that way. If it had been an afternoon session, she would have spent all morning worried about how she would make it there without being spotted by the enemy. Morning sessions reduced dwelling time.

***

Sitting in his waiting room her head continued to pound.

The tablets did nothing to ease her pain. *Next time maybe don't drink so much.* But she smiled as she recalled watching Arthur's life fall apart.

"Are you okay?" Hilary asked.

Bridget nodded. "Had a rough night but I'm sure Daniel will help me."

Before Hilary had a chance to reply, Daniel opened his office door and greeted Bridget with a smile. "Good morning, shall we talk?"

His welcoming smile was a sight for literally sore eyes. Bridget brushed past him inhaling the sweet scent of his aftershave. Flopping down in the familiar corner chair, she sighed. She was with Daniel; everything appeared better when she was with Daniel.

They'd been talking for about twenty minutes when Bridget admitted to her revenge on Arthur Fuller. She smiled as she spoke of watching his life fall apart, how she watched him collapse to the ground. She was pleased with the success of her mission. Then she told him of her visit from Zack. She was concerned Zack or Sandra would tell others of their suspicions.

Daniel lent over and placed his warm hand gently upon hers. Tears welled in her eyes.

"Come away with me…" he blurted.

"What?" Bridget replied, not sure she had heard him correctly.

"Come away with me."

"Where to?"

"I have a cabin in the country. It's only just over an hour away from here. It's secluded, in a quiet valley. My closest neighbour lives two valleys over. The break would do you wonders. There is fresh air. There is a small stream where you could do some fishing. Trails to wander. Maybe that's what you need. The scenery is beautiful. Just some time away to relax."

Bridget looked at Daniel. She wanted to leap from her chair and say yes but she didn't want to appear desperate.

"When was the last time you took time out for yourself. You need to do things that create pleasure. Take me for example, I love my job but I need an outlet. I escape to my cabin. I have hobbies. I am also completing a course in massage. It's healthy to have an outlet. Something to distract our minds from everyday life. Everyone needs a break." He gave her another smile. "I'll tell you what… no pressure, just think about it. I am going there this Saturday. If you want to come along, let me know and I will pick you up on the way. Just an overnight stay."

Bridget nodded. "I will, thanks. I will think about it. As you say maybe the break would do me good. Fresh country air might help clear my head."

Chapter Twelve

Driving along Daniel glanced towards Bridget and smiled. "I'm so glad you decided to come along. You're going to love it. You'll have space to wander around. Space to think and you needn't worry about a thing. I have enough food to feed an army," he said with a laugh.

Bridget smiled but remained silent. She felt safe near Daniel, and soon they'd be at his cabin. Her mobile phone was turned off. No one knew where she was going. *A weekend with delightful company, peace and complete rest will work wonders.* However, she couldn't help but think about what Zack had said the other night. She worried that Samuel Easton and Arthur Fuller might suspect she had a hand in their recent turn of events. Surely they wouldn't think of her, she hadn't been around for years. Why would she even cross their minds? Samuel's grass attack could have been carried out by anyone. As for Arthur, it was only a matter of time before his sleeping around caught up with him. Liars and cheats were always exposed.

The car slowed as Daniel announced their arrival at his property. Turning onto a concealed and darkened dirt track he placed the car into park. Bridget scanned her surrounds as he jumped from the car with great enthusiasm and opened a locked wrought-iron gate, locking it behind them once they were through. He was right; the place was secluded. At the almost hidden driveway, a large red and white sign clearly stated: Private Property – No Trespassing.

Bridget coughed nervously and cast her eyes up the long and narrow rocky road ahead. Her mouth was dry; a drink from her water bottle did little to alleviate her anxiety. Where was he taking her? She knew she had feelings and desires for him she longed to explore, but did she really know the man she had been talking to for years? His property was far more secluded than she'd imagined. *He could be a madman.* He could do anything to her and no one would hear her screams. No one would know where she was. He could murder her and dump her body. Her remains would never be found. Maybe she should have told someone where she was going.

Out of the corner of her eye, she studied his face. He didn't look like a madman, but then again what did a madman look like? He was muscular, and could easily overpower her. Was this a rocky road to disaster?

As they drove the track, there was no sight of any dwellings. She couldn't recall seeing another house for miles. They were surrounded by trees and mountainous terrain. Maybe this wasn't the first time he'd lured an unsuspecting victim to their death. How would she ever find her way back to civilisation if she needed to escape? She closed her eyes and tried to dispel her fears as ridiculous. With a deep breath, she opened her eyes and attempted to focus on the beauty of her surrounds. She knew all too well how fear had the power to constrict and control.

Thousands of giant pine trees lay before them, underneath them lie a soft and beautiful carpet of pine needles. Winding down her window she inhaled the fresh cool air. The smell of damp earth combined with strong coniferous scents, filled her lungs and relaxed her mind. She listened to the ruffling of the pine needles as the branches swayed in the breeze. The trees reached up high and blocked out most of the sunlight. Their limbs spread up and over the car like huge arms that created a welcoming tunnel. She smiled and reassured herself all would be fine.

Easing over bumps and trenches, it took a good ten minutes to reach Daniel's cabin. Bridget sat in the passenger seat, one hand clinging to the door as Daniel reassured her of her safety.

"An untrained person may have a problem coming up here, if you don't know where to go you could easily roll your car but I've driven this track many times. Could do it with my eyes closed and still arrive safely. That's what I love about it out here. While we're close to the city, the hills and valleys, the steep terrain and running streams, the endless trees and dense bushland give us a sense of seclusion. Some of the properties that border my far boundary are even more secluded and those people are a little odd." He paused and chuckled looking towards Bridget. "I think living off the grid has warped them slightly, but they tend to keep to themselves. I know you're going to love this place as much as I do," he said.

Unpacking the car took minutes. Opening the front door to the cabin, Bridget's senses were again sent into overdrive. This time a mix of a musty odour, stale cigarettes and dust danced up her nostrils. She sneezed. Daniel dropped his bags to the floor and hit the roof.

"Fuck! I am fucking *sick* of bastards thinking they can be disrespectful and just get away with things," he snapped.

Bridget stood dumbfounded; her eyes and mouth wide open. "What? Who?" she asked.

He shook his head; eyes narrowed, his nostrils flared. His jaw clenched and his hands balled into fists. She'd never seen him angry.

"Guys who think they can get away with anything."

"Who are you talking about?" she said. "What's wrong?"

"The cabin smells like a fucken ashtray. I told them they couldn't smoke inside. They asked me specifically. I told them no," he began to pace. He strode to the stone fireplace and picked up a glass filled with dirty water and cigarette butts that rested precariously on the mantle. "Well they won't be getting their deposit back." He groaned as he passed a gouge in the oak paneling of the wall. He examined scuffmarks on the oak floorboards and spotted a cigarette burn on the couch. "And they'd better not think about coming back. *Bastards*. I can't stand people who think they have the right to disrespect others," he snarled.

"It's okay," Bridget said, trying to calm him. "We'll open the doors and windows. We can air it out. Daniel, don't worry, it will be okay."

Daniel nodded, then gave her a smile. "Sorry. I didn't mean to snap, they just make me so mad. I rent it out to make a bit of money but I always insist there's no smoking inside. Some people don't like to walk into a place smelling like a dirty old ashtray. I have rules for a reason. Sorry."

Bridget stood silent as Daniel walked into the kitchen, tipped the water out of the glass and threw the butts into the bin then placed the empty glass in the sink. Her eyes scanned the room. The focal point of the downstairs lounge was a large stone fireplace set in the centre of the back wall. To the left was a small kitchen. The interior and furnishings were slightly outdated and basic, yet comfortable. It had a welcoming feel, relaxing. Daniel returned to her side, smiled then picked up his bags and showed Bridget up the stairs to a bedroom at the end of the hallway. It would be hers for the night. His bedroom was closer to the top of the stairs, and there was a bathroom separating the two rooms. Her bedroom was simply decorated. A wooden queen sized bed sat opposite the door with matching bedside tables. A quilt in warm berry tones complimented the rich timber and created an effortlessly romantic look. A large framed wall quote hung over the bed, "Do what you love every day." In the corner, between the bedroom window and an antique dressing table was a Charles of London chair, which provided a cosy vintage meets rustic styling. Bridget unpacked her bags and returned downstairs.

They opened the windows to air the place. Daniel made them a snack of dips, mixed cheeses, fresh fruits and crackers. Relaxing on the front porch they enjoyed the afternoon sun. Wind whispered through the trees as cockatoos swooped down and collected the bread they had tossed out for them.

They took a stroll down to the stream and over a rocky outcrop that ended where the pine trees commenced. By the time they returned to the cabin most of the cigarette odour had gone, and Bridget could feel every muscle in her legs.

As they sipped on white wine, warm sunlight danced on Bridget's face as she watched Daniel prepare a barbecue. He insisted he was there to take care of her every need, that it was her time to relax and enjoy. It was so peaceful and so she strolled around the clearing near the cabin picking flowers along her way. She returned with a bright bunch of yellow daffodils.

"I love it here," she said, unable to stop a smile. "I'm so glad I came. Are you getting a pool put in around the back?"

Daniel smiled when she handed him the flowers and laughed at her question. "No, nothing as exciting as a pool. Just a new water tank. I'm afraid my old tank was on its last legs so I'm going for a new model. It's completely underground so I can utilise all that space too. It seems so wasted around there. I may even put a back porch on the place, which I think will be nice with the morning sun. But I do have a pool at my place in the city," he said and took a sip of his wine. "Maybe you'd like to come over for a dip one day."

Bridget smiled. "A dip would be nice," she said. *A skinny dip would be even better.*

A cool breeze delivered a darkening night sky as they ate dinner. They retreated inside for an enjoyable evening of soft music and idle talk. The fresh air was soothing. An afternoon of exploring, eating and talking had been exhausting and so they hugged and said their good nights.

Bridget sank into the soft mattress, and snuggled beneath the warm blankets. Her room was slightly cool, so she pulled the covers up and wrapped them firmly beneath her chin. She closed her eyes and listened to the sounds of the night. There were no cars or traffic and no streetlights, just the gentle rustle of the breeze within the trees and total blackness. She was asleep in minutes.

CHAPTER THIRTEEN

“No! No! Nooo!”

Blood curdling screams ripped through the cabin. Daniel sprung up in his bed. Everything was pitch black. Another scream tore through the night. He lunged for his bedside light and knocked it to the floor. Fumbling around he found the switch.

“Get off me! Stop! Nooo!”

Glass shattered.

Daniel leaped from his bed, and dashed towards the bedroom at the end of the hall. Someone was in the cabin. Someone was attacking Bridget. Adrenalin kicked in. Another scream shattered through the cabin.

“Help meeee! He’s going to kill me! Help!”

Daniel burst through the door and hurtled towards the bed. His foot caught on something and he crashed to the floor, sliding along the polished floorboards. His head slammed into the end of the wooden bed frame. Dazed, he jumped to his feet, fists raised for the onslaught of her attacker. Bridget thrashed around on the bed. Daniel’s eyes darted about, as he tried to work out what was what. The only light snuck in from the hallway. His heart raced. The bedroom window was open. Where was her attacker?

“Nooo!” Bridget screamed. The kicking and thrashing continued. The attacker was on the bed. The blankets distorted everything. Daniel hesitated.

The blankets fell to the floor. "He's going to kill me!" Bridget punched wildly into the air. She was fighting an invisible attacker. One who assaulted when she was most vulnerable. When no escape was possible. No wonder she feared sleeping. It was when she slept he struck.

Daniel grabbed her arms then threw his legs around hers "It's okay. You're okay, Bridget. It's Daniel. I'm here. He can't hurt you anymore. Shhh. I'll protect you. Bridget it's me. It's Daniel. Listen to my voice. You have nothing to fear," he said gently.

Her thrashing slowly calmed as he continued to talk to her.

"It's okay. It's going to be okay."

He hugged her tightly. Her breath was ragged against his neck. Her body tense. Her panic stricken eyes finally met his. Daniel clung to her. His heart raced. Her heart raced.

So many clients had described their nightmares, but nothing could have prepared him for this. Bridget had appeared wild. Clawing for freedom. How had she not hurt herself? He wrapped his arms around her, holding her close. Her breathing settled. Daniel closed his eyes. Bridget released a loud sigh then began to sob. The rise and fall of her chest made him open his eyes, but as he held her tight, her sobbing increased.

"Are you okay?" he whispered.

Bridget stared at him, eyes wide with confusion.

"What are you doing?" she asked.

"You were having a nightmare."

"What are you doing in my bed?"

"I came to help you. You were having a nightmare. You screamed. Something smashed. I thought you were being attacked," he said. "I did nothing wrong. I didn't take advantage of you," he said defensively. "I came to help. I only wanted to help."

Bridget burst into tears. "Why didn't I meet you years

ago?"

"You did. It's me – Daniel," he replied, unsure if she was awake or talking in her sleep.

"I know who you are," she snapped, "I don't mean like that. I'm talking about wasted time. Why did we have to meet when my life was shit? I've wasted years. I can't escape their clutches. Those bastards stole my life," she hissed.

"They can't hurt you anymore. I won't let them. I'm here now. I'm not going anywhere. I promise."

Bridget freed herself from his hold and clambered from the bed to turn on the light. Daniel stayed on the bed. He wanted to go to her side, but didn't want to crowd her. Bridget shivered; walked to the window and closed it ensuring it was locked. While the night air was cool, there was no breeze, only a dark stillness. She began pacing. Daniel sat still. Her nightmares concerned him, and he wished he could do more to ease her pain. For now he would listen. She began to flick her fingers, as her frustration increased – it was a tell he'd picked up on in the therapy sessions. She clasped her hands together then placed them upon her head. Tears began to well in her eyes.

"You don't understand. Something terrible happened and I couldn't change it. I dealt with it, but I couldn't fix it. I didn't stop it. I couldn't stop it. I just wish I could go back in time so I could stop it from happening." She shook her head. "My guilt follows me. It overshadows all I do. I'm so confused. I've lost so much time. The trauma, my heartache, all the pain and for what? I hate them *so* much. I shut down. I shut off. I can't even recall large chunks of my life." She looked at him then. "I know you've explained it was my brain's way of helping me cope. But I just can't stop thinking about what they did. They're heartless, thieving bastards, all of them." She clenched her hands, and her dark eyes darkened further with her fury. "They make me *sick*. I know I'm far better than what I was. But will I ever feel better? What will it take?" She let out a shaky breath and dropped her head. "I'm ashamed by how I feel. The way I think about revenge sometimes scares me. Would my pain end if they were dead? I don't know… I just don't know. I never…" She shook her head again. "I believe I'm a good person. But if I saw them on fire, I wouldn't even be bothered to spit on the flames. If I heard they were dead I'd cheer. Does that make me a bad person?"

The frustration in Bridget's words, and the pain on her face, made him choose his words carefully as she looked to him for answers. Her eyes were dull and teary. Her brow furrowed; lips quivered.

"Of course you're not a bad person, Bridget," he said gently. "You care. It's what they did that makes you feel this way. You have nothing to be guilty or ashamed of. They'll get what they deserve. All of them will pay for their wrongdoings, it's called Karma. You *must* trust me."

Daniel climbed off the bed maintaining eye contact with Bridget. There was a red mark on the side of her face where she must have struck herself in her panic. He placed his hands gently around her waist and slowly pulled her towards him. She gave him a half smile as they faced each other. Daniel stepped closer then gently wiped the tears from her cheeks. He smiled, his hands clasped behind her back. He gazed into her eyes, winked, then brushed his lips across hers. She returned the kiss.

Bridget hesitated then leaned back to gaze into his eyes. He felt her anxiety as well as his own. He could feel the warmth of her breath, and he wondered if she felt as nervous as he did. He gave her a small smile.

The scent of her sweet perfume filled him. He wanted to feel the softness of her lips again, the warmth of her body against his. Bridget's shoulders raised as she took a deep breath. He could tell she was having doubts. A step forward, and her body was against his. He could wait no longer. He sank into the sensuousness of her lips, his hands moving gently over her body and pulling her closer. He kissed down her neck, soft moans escaping him.

"I want you…" he whispered. "But not like this. I never want you to think I've taken advantage of you. You need sleep. We need to talk about where things are going between us. You know I have feelings for you. But tonight we should sleep." He kissed her neck again. "I'll stay with you until you fall asleep. We don't need to rush."

Bridget nodded. "I want you too, but I'm exhausted. I just wish I could sleep," she sighed.

He stepped back and looked into her eyes. Smiled. Kissed her again. "You need to get some rest. Why don't you climb back into bed and I'll get something that will help you sleep."

With a nod she climbed into bed while he went downstairs. When he returned, she was sitting up in bed, waiting.

He handed her the glass and the pill. "What is it?" she asked.

"A Mogadon, it will help you sleep," he said with a smile.

Taking a sip of water she popped the pill in her mouth and swallowed. She handed him the glass and scooted down into the bed.

Daniel walked over and stared out of the window. All was dark. All was quiet. They were alone. He placed the glass onto the bedside table and climbed onto the other side of the bed.

"I'll stay here with you," he said. "I'll keep you safe, Bridget." Leaning over he gently kissed her cheek as he wrapped his arm around her, listening to her breathe. Before he knew it, her breathing changed to the steady cadence of sleep. Daniel smiled at her light snoring. She wouldn't wake. The tablet would keep her sleeping well beyond sunrise.

Curling up he absorbed her warmth. Their closeness only added to his emotional struggle, swallowing became difficult. Sleep, how could he sleep when all he thought about was Bridget? Tightness and a slight ache enveloped his shoulders. Bridget was forbidden. Staring into the darkness, he thought about the tender kiss they had shared, and the softness of her skin. *I love her. I always have but I can't have her.* Blinking away tears, he closed his eyes. *How can something be so wrong when it feels so right?*

CHAPTER FOURTEEN

Positioned in the corner of the dining room, she sat. Watched. Waited. She had prime position. Everything had been building to his moment. No one could venture behind her. No one would enter or leave without her knowledge. Five minutes passed. She rested. Yet, she was not complacent. She scanned. She listened. People were bunched together in groups talking, eating and drinking. A small gathering of seven were celebrating a birthday. A lone candle flickered atop the birthday cake as those around the old lady burst into song. She blew out the candle in one breath. A loud group of young guys in dirty jerseys congregated near the bar at the far end of the room discussing tactics for their weekend match.

Five more minutes passed. Then ten. She was patient. Perseverance and restraint was a must. The dining room was full. No one would take any notice of a single woman eating alone.

Her target stood to the right of the footballers. He guzzled his beer. The sight of him almost made her throw up her dinner. Her heart beat wildly in her chest. Anticipation was a sickeningly wonderful thing. He stood with his two mates. All three were familiar to her. Soon the other two would leave, and he would be alone. Stagger home he would. That was when she would strike. She had rehearsed her moves. Everything was going according to plan.

These days she liked to refer to herself as a lioness. Not to be confused with a cougar, the type of older woman who searched out younger men to gain sexual gratification. Bridget was far from being an older woman. Rather, she was a hunter who stalked her prey.

Her wig hovered just above her shoulders, and her make-up was unblemished. The blood red lipstick applied to her lips, a reflection of her intentions. Revenge the only thing on her mind. Her unsuspecting victim was yet to make her acquaintance. He won't recognise her, but she needed to get close. The adrenaline rush was invigorating. The sense of being alive was addictive. Her life now had purpose. This one had to be bigger and better than the last.

She checked the clock on the wall. Less than an hour. She knew they would play a game of pool. They always did. She watched where they placed their glasses. Normally they would move to the vacant tables left of where they stood.

Finally they moved. Nerves tingled up her spine. She could feel the pulse in her forehead. This attack was far more daring than her last. They placed their drinks on the table. She scanned the room. Her heart pounded in her chest, so much so she believed others could hear its rapid beat. Short and shallow breaths escaped her. Her lips became dry, her mouth void of all moisture. She struggled to swallow.

The three turned their backs on the table and began to set up their game of pool. *Time to strike*. Her strides were nonchalant between the dining tables, heading towards the ladies bathroom beyond them. She watched their every move. Their focus was on the pool balls. Her focus darted between them, the table on which their drinks sat, and the bathroom. She slipped her hand from her pocket.

Now or never. She released a pouch of white powder into the glass of her target. Her move went unnoticed as she continued on her path to the bathroom. Once inside, she dashed into the cubicle and slammed the door behind her, locked it, then collapsed onto the toilet seat.

Overwhelmed by what she'd just done, she burst into tears.

Stage one of her mission was complete.

CHAPTER FIFTEEN

Hidden away in the bathroom cubicle, warm tears streamed down Bridget's face as she clutched her pounding chest. A strong disinfectant odour bombarded her. Her eyes wandered over the graffiti on the walls. Why would people plaster their names and telephone numbers on the walls of toilets? Were they done by the individual themselves or was it the work of someone else playing a joke or being spiteful? The walls offered no answers, and she was not interested in calling any of the numbers to find out. Instead, she sat in silence. Alone. She needed to pull herself together. The two other cubicles had been vacant when she burst through the main door, and no one had entered behind. She couldn't believe what she'd just done, but Pierre Rainer deserved everything he got. The pain he'd inflicted upon her was immeasurable. He was the power behind the force, the mastermind behind her suffering – a narcissistic bastard. He terrified her.

This wasn't the first time she'd taken refuge in a toilet cubicle, but it would be the last.

Pierre was an arrogant piece of work. A tall, bull-necked, barrel-chested, burly bloke who wore his clothes too tight and used his size to terrorise. A stand-over guy with a short fuse. His behaviour was what you may expect of a childish brat throwing a temper tantrum, only with Pierre came the added threats of violence. He was a bully. And at his age, should have known better.

Strutting around the office, he considered himself somewhat of a ladies man, a stud. Yet in reality most female employees viewed him as a dog that doused himself in copious amounts of cheap, overpowering cologne – a washed-up has-been. Approaching his mid-forties, Pierre was out to prove that age would not prevent him from having any woman he chose. In his mind, everything revolved around him. Sporting a cropped-cut hairstyle; nothing could disguise his receding hairline and those increasing flecks of grey. Had he shed some of those unwanted pounds, Bridget was sure he would have looked much older, as it was his oval face and puffed out cheeks that helped smooth his wrinkles.

Her first thought when she was introduced to him was that he looked like a puffer fish… with brown, shifty, pig eyes and a snarly mouth to match. During her job interview she had been warned about his insubordination. To Pierre, she was the enemy. Not only was she his new manager, but she was female to boot.

"Nice to meet you," she'd said, attempting to shake his hand.

"I'm busy," he'd huffed, as he'd stormed by. "We'll see how long you last," he'd mumbled, as their shoulders collided.

Raising her eyebrows in shock she'd turned to the Regional Manager, Richard West, whose face had been aglow. "He must be having a bad day, he'll be okay," he'd said, trying to convince her all would be fine, but not making eye contact as he'd pulled at his jacket and ushered her forward without delay. She should have taken this encounter as a warning. Pierre didn't take kindly to women telling him what to do. How could he ever be expected to take orders from a manager who didn't possess a dingle-dangle and two sinkers? He was a misogynist, and Bridget had heard stories of previous female managers who'd succumbed to his antics. Yet, she'd been assured all would be fine.

Senior management had addressed his behaviour and given

her their commitment to being dedicated to strong business ethics; teamwork, support and respect, fairness, integrity and uncompromising standards regarding equality and diversity. Heck, she'd even received a personal assurance from Mr Wolf, the owner of Wolf Industries.

"I will not tolerate workplace harassment," he'd stated, as he'd slammed his fist onto the table. "We provide a safe work environment for everyone and if people do not adhere to our high standards and respect others they know where the door is."

Hearing those supporting words had provided confidence that all those stories were a thing of the past.

They say a leopard doesn't change its spots, however she was assured Pierre's aggression would be controlled by the rules and policies set in place to protect all. That was what she'd been led to believe. What a joke. Her assurances had been short lived. Their words were hollow, and her complaints fell on deaf ears. They may as well have thrown her into the cage for they sure as hell weren't interested in controlling or addressing the multitude of reports she'd submitted regarding Pierre's insubordination.

Nicknamed 'The Hulk', Pierre was a man on a mission. A narcissistic arsehole, who inflicted intentional cruelty upon others. He was a hunter who used force, threats and aggression to instil fear, terrorise and hurt. His mission was to destroy. His behaviour was repeated and habitual. He was a bully who felt empowered by demeaning others. He used his size to intimidate, and with his almost Neanderthal features, silently ruled the workplace. He had done so for years, and Bridget's appointment would not stop him.

She often wondered if his nickname was a reflection of his size, his power or the level of aggression he was capable of displaying. Pierre Rainer was the Union delegate and no one wanted to upset the Union. Upsetting the Union could result in strikes, and strikes meant lost revenue. Money makes the world go round, and Bridget soon learnt that money came first and foremost. It was far more important than the welfare of employees. Pierre Rainer knew this and used the company's greed as his ally. He was untouchable. And Bridget was in his firing line.

Bridget shivered as she recalled one of his most violent attacks. He had cut her off as she'd attempted to escape to the ladies toilets. She had not made it to safety. No one saw. No one heard. No one would believe her against Pierre Rainer, and that would only be if she dared to speak up against him. She had never spoken of his ambush.

The squeaking of the toilet door brought her back to the now. She closed her eyes and fought back tears. She hated him. She wanted to annihilate him. So sickening, so wicked had some of his acts been that she'd never told a soul. He repulsed—

Leaping from the toilet Bridget swung around just in time, flipping the lid as she lost the contents of her stomach. This only fuelled her anger, fired up her determination.

Pierre Rainer was going to pay. She would bring this master manipulator to his knees.

CHAPTER SIXTEEN

Bridget sat, her teeth clenched as she wiped away her tears. Hate filled her heart. She was alone again. Determined to settle the score. Only when the wrongs had been righted, would she be able to move forward. There were two types of people who sought revenge – those who desired instant gratification, and those who played the long game. There was little doubt which she was. Forgiveness was not an option. She had created a method so meticulous in its planning that she would finally gain retribution.

Vengeance will be mine.

Rising to her feet she exited the cubicle and began to pace back and forth in front of the wash basins. Rage burned through her; her anger all consuming. They did this to her; it was only fair she returned the favour. Her life had been destroyed. Her happiness shattered. They hadn't given her a second thought. So why should she spare them any pain?

Checking her watch, it was time to return to the bar. Doubt began to creep in, and she wondered if she should continue. Would revenge offer the sense of fulfilment she so desired? What would happen if she were caught? Overwhelmed by fear, she began to sweat and shake. Procrastinating would get her nowhere. She had to return to the bar and see it through. She wiped her brow, pulled herself together, and stepped from behind her walls of protection.

She spotted him immediately, and she moved unnoticed towards the front door as her target drank down the last of his beer. He raised his hand to his mouth and yawned. The three friends would soon part company, and Pierre Rainer would be alone.

She hadn't forgotten his haunting image or the warmth and rank smell of his breath. Not his spit hitting her in the face, nor the strength of his shoves and the evil in his eyes that had cut deep into her soul. Soon the tables would turn. Pierre Rainer would come face to face with his demons from the past.

She dashed to her car and drove to her strike zone. All was dark. All was quiet.

Watching him stagger towards her, Bridget began to feel sick. Her nerves intensified. A large lump formed in her throat. What if he spotted her? What if someone heard? What if someone witnessed her attack? Someone could phone the police. Someone could come to his aid. She was shaking. Her hands were sweaty beneath the gloves. She clenched the tyre iron as she peered through the bush she was hiding behind; the balaclava she wore limited her vision.

He staggered closer. He stumbled; wiped his eyes. Soon he would be level with her. *No turning back.*

Bridget had done her homework. Pierre's partner, Judy, was away for the weekend competing in a softball championship. His absence would go unnoticed. His feet crunched against the loose gravel on the path. The scraping of his leather shoes neared. She froze. Held her breath.

He staggered past.

A quick glance around. They were alone.

She rose; her steps cat-like. She approached from behind, both hands clasped tightly on tyre iron. She struck. Contact.

A loud crack filled her ears. He hit the ground with a thud. Blood seeped from his head, and Bridget feared she'd killed him. She dashed to his side; her mission far from over. *Alive.* She grabbed his wrists, checked again that they were still alone then began to drag him into her car. His clothes scrapped along the path, and sounded like sandpaper rubbing over a rough surface. His flabby body was heavy, but her weight lifting had prepared her. She was determined to win. Her attack had been timed perfectly, and finally she had his body next to her back tyre.

It took a matter of moments to get his limp body onto the back seat. He was out cold, and would remain that way for hours. The drugs she'd slipped into his drink would see to that. She closed his door, placed the tyre iron in her boot, along with her gloves and balaclava then drove home.

Bridget's staging needed to be precise. Turning into her driveway she smiled as she spotted her wheelbarrow. It sat ready near her rear side entrance. Unloading Pierre was easier than she had anticipated. A long board extended over the three steps into her house, and she wheeled Pierre inside.

Bridget smiled as she dumped him on the floor then tied him up. Her plan was coming together. She left him alone and bound on the floor. Pierre had never been inside her house, and even if he woke he wouldn't recognise his surrounding.

CHAPTER SEVENTEEN

B ridget couldn't wait till tomorrow. It was still dark outside. The street in front of her house was quiet and deserted. There were still several hours before she had to leave. She smiled. For once her sleepless night was not the result of nightmares. Checks were made then double and triple checks. Everything was planned. Everything needed to be precise. Black balaclava, a large and long black jacket, latex surgical gloves, overalls, electrical tape, bolt cutters, a hammer, two large d-shackles and the exact length of heavy gauge chain. Chain she had driven over one hundred kilometres to collect from a marine supply warehouse the day before. She smiled; it was all coming together. All the bits and pieces required for inflicting bodily pain were at her fingertips. More so than all these items, she had the element of surprise. Pierre Rainer wouldn't know what had hit him when he came to.

Daniel's words played over in her mind; *"They will get what they deserve."*

No one would be so naive to think life would be a fairytale, but few would anticipate a terrorising attack just around the corner, Pierre Rainer included. Life followed a natural progression, for every action there is a reaction. Unexpected situations resulted in plans being changed. The road travelled was not always smooth. Pierre Rainer would soon discover the truth of this.

Bridget could barely contain her excitement. She bit her

fingernails and paced around the room. She had to see if he had moved.

Pulling the balaclava over her head she peeked around the corner, and looked down at his limp body. He was defenceless. His face was expressionless. She'd worn the same expression when she'd pleaded with him to spare her. He didn't listen. He hadn't cared. She had begged him to leave her alone. She prayed he would stop. He did not.

The sight of him made her sick. She couldn't stand to look at him. Anger flooded her, she stepped closer and she pounded her boot into his face with all her might. His nose shattered. He moaned and remained unconscious. Blood flowed to the floor. Bridget huffed and left the room; she would clean the mess later. She removed her balaclava. She sucked in deep breaths. Her relief was slight. Her waiting game had commenced.

One hour passed then another before Pierre began to moan and groan. Finally, he was coming to. She was relieved. She had become bored with the waiting. Her mission was to inflict so much pain and fear he would never forget. Doing so required him to be awake. She wanted his horror to haunt his every waking hour. Disturbing nightmares would wake him from the deepest sleep. She would be his worst nightmare, just as he had been hers. She would destroy him.

His eyes opened. Bridget froze. Glaring at him propelled her thoughts back to one of his painful attacks. On that occasion they had been alone. She was frozen stiff. She stared straight ahead into his blackened eyes. Short shallow breaths escaped her. She was not game to blink. It was like staring into the eyes of a wild animal, his next move unpredictable. Her back was planted firmly against the hard cold surface of the brick wall in the parking garage. Her heart hammered in her chest. If only she had been more alert, she should never have allowed herself to be alone with him. She began to pray someone might enter. Surely someone would hear his raised voice, his ranting insults, his thunderous threats. She could feel the warmth of his breath on her face.

"You had better watch your back you bitch." He shoved his thick finger against her chest.

"What?"

"You heard me," he snarled. "You've been warned." He poked harder.

How much longer can I take this? Why won't anyone help me? He was a monster of a man. She squirmed within his shadow, wishing he would stop, nausea swirling in her gut. But all the wishing in the world wasn't going to get her anywhere. This wasn't the first attack and she was sure it wouldn't be the last. *I can't be sick. I must be brave. If I move now then he'll win. I can't let him believe he's won I must maintain my illusion of calmness. I've worked hard to earn my position in this company and no bully is going to force me to walk away.*

Pierre towered over her. He had to be at least six foot tall and nearing 300 pounds. His finger pointed wildly inches from her face. She bit back a scream. Fought back tears. It was imperative she hid her fear.

"I am fucking *sick* of you. You are nothing more than a thundercunt, a slaggy fucktard. Everyone hates you. You're a loser and we don't want you here. Do you hear me? When are you going to get that through your thick head? We don't need a skittle tit bitch. I'm going to organise a vote of no confidence. Everyone will say you can't do your job. I'll go to management and you'll be out that door. It doesn't matter what you say to them. They won't believe you. I have the numbers behind me. I have witnesses. I run this place not you, you Adolf Titler, thundercunt whore," he spat.

Bridget stood petrified. She had no doubt about his intentions. All her efforts to gain assistance from senior management had failed. She was alone and in a second he was gone. His overpowering aftershave lingered, as did his hateful words.

And now, they were again alone. Oh, how the tables had

turned!

Pierre groaned and began thrashing on the floor. He blinked rapidly, obviously trying to focus. She was sure the last thing he remembered was walking home.

"What's happening?" he groaned.

Bridget's attention returned to the room. Pierre kept blinking. His head began to thrash. His eyes darted. Bridget could not change the past. She had to deal with what lay before her. This time *she* was in control.

Pierre went ballistic, yelling and screaming, when he realised he was bound. He struggled and strained. Sweat ran from his brow, his face contorted with fury. He flipped from side to side.

Bridget stood to the right of the door, near the window that had been sealed closed. It was covered with foam board and heavy insulated material to sound proof what would be his holding pen. In fact, the whole room was a mass of white foam insulation sheeting. No one would hear his cries. Escape was impossible. Hog-tied, rope extended from his ankles and ran firmly along his legs twisting around his wrists. A slipknot had been created wrapping around his throat. The more he struggled, the more it restricted his air supply – it was amazing what you could learn on the Internet.

He stared towards her. "Who are you?" he screeched. "What do you want?" His voice echoed around the room. His kicking halted, as he realised the consequences of his actions.

A masked Bridget stood still, and silent. She was in control. Her large coat with padded shoulders, full-length overalls, gloves and heavy combat boots concealed her identity.

"Who are you? Show yourself you weak bastard, be a man and face me," he spat.

Looking down upon him, she felt pity and revulsion in equal measure. Echoes of advice she had received from those in charge at Wolf Industries danced around in her mind, *"Don't let them see they have affected you or that will give them greater power."*

She turned her back on him. She remained silent. She walked out of the room. The door slammed behind her. Inside his yelling continued. Outside it was barely a muffle. She removed her mask and gasped for air. *Oh my god what am I doing?*

There was no going back.

CHAPTER EIGHTEEN

Gasping for air, Bridget felt the warmth of a tear slip from the corner of her eye. A wave of nausea gurgled up from the pit of her stomach. She inhaled deeply as a twinge tickled her nostrils. *What the hell am I doing?* She swallowed hard. Fear from events of the past wouldn't dictate her life. Painful memories infiltrated her mind but they would never win. Many people experienced different struggles in life, but with support, love, friendship and determination they could overcome hurdles. She would be no different. Pierre Rainer would not dictate her future happiness. He had to be dealt with.

We cannot live in the past; we can only acknowledge what has happened and look to the future with hope.

Taking a deep breath she regathered herself. *Focus.* Ruminating over past experiences would get her nowhere. She pulled her balaclava down over her face and collected the hammer she had placed on the floor. Another deep breath and she returned to his holding pen.

Closing the door behind her, Pierre squirmed on the floor. It was time for him to be moved. The next phase of her operation had to be completed before sunrise. There was no time for delay. She lunged forward, and struck him on the side of the head. *Thud.* Pierre's body went limp.

Blood seeped from his wound. She checked his pulse. He

was alive. She grabbed him under his arms, and pulled him up and lent his body next to the wall. She gathered her trusty wheelbarrow, wrenched his senseless body into it and wheeled him outside and down into her garage. Stars blanketed the sky. Everything was quiet. Everything was still. The only sound her rapid heartbeat.

She closed the garage door behind her. No one would suspect a thing.

Bridget was committed to sharing experiences with her partners, and Zack had had a passion for restoring old cars. They had enjoyed countless hours tinkering together, and one task she had been assigned was operating the electronic winch. It was vital she knew how to operate it so she could move the engine into position while Zack completed the required adjustments and fixings. Zack had forgotten about it when they'd discussed who would get what in their separation. Suspended from the roof of the garage, it was a vital piece of equipment for this stage of her operation.

Bridget wheeled Pierre into position then pushed him forward, his forehead striking his knees that rested on the edge of the wheelbarrow. He moaned.

Bridget grabbed his head and studied his face – still unconscious. She sighed with relief then wrapped the winch cable around his chest ensuring she secured the hook around the cable. Dashing to the controls, she pushed the button. The motor whirled. Pierre began to lift from the wheelbarrow, and Bridget smiled.

Pierre's feet dangled in the air, and Bridget released the button then manoeuvred Pierre's body over her target before using the button to lower him again. His body slowly dropped. The cable became slack. She retrieved her stepladder from the garage wall and climbed into Zack's boat and released the cable from around Pierre's waist. Next, she untied the ropes that had bound his wrists, feet and neck. Gagging him with an old rag, she secured it in place with duct tape. Cable ties held his wrists together, and she wrapped chain around his ankles, ensuring it was securely connected to the long length of chain she had coiled on the deck of the boat. Everything was as she had planned. Covering his body with a large green canvas tarp, she flung a long length of old rope over it – no one would suspect a body was concealed beneath. She smiled. She chuckled. She fist-punched the air. This phase of her operation was complete.

Pierre Rainer was going to get more than he bargained for.

Bridget climbed down from the boat and returned the stepladder to the wall then checked her watch. Everything was running to time. She still had a couple of hours before the sun would rise. Her car was packed. The only thing that remained was to connect the car to the trailer and she would be on her way. What she deserved now though, was a nice hot cup of coffee. Every great achievement should be celebrated with a reward. A hot cup of coffee would be wonderful.

Bridget sipped her coffee, as she paced her kitchen. The combination of blows to his head and drugs she had slipped into his drink would see Pierre Rainer asleep for a few hours yet. Hours in which she would travel to the seaside.

Her fun was only just beginning.

His nightmare had only started.

CHAPTER NINETEEN

Daybreak delivered a stormy sky and ocean swell. A bank of ominous looking clouds sat on the horizon. Weather forecasts predicted afternoon thunderstorms. Strong winds and white caps on the ocean discouraged the recreational fishers, but Bridget would not be deterred. They were alone on the water. The ocean was theirs. Rolling waves rocked against Zack's boat. The swell had picked up, pounding waves smashed into the rocks. Cool, salty sea spray hit Bridget's face and danced on her tongue. The sandstone cliffs around The Gap on the South Head peninsula of Watsons Bay sat in the distance. She turned off the engine and lowered the anchor. She put her balaclava on and confirmed everything was as she'd planned.

She grabbed the old red bucket; they used as an at-sea toilet, and reached over the side of the boat and filled it with the icy water. Pierre was flat on his back. His white shirt was speckled with blood. The right knee of his jeans had been ripped when she'd moved him. His pants were rolled up his calves, and she'd removed his shoes and socks. His gag was now gone, and he was still secured by cable ties and the chain. Time for him to wake.

Bridget hadn't seen Pierre in years, though the thought of him had never left her mind. Today was the day of reckoning. She threw the bucket of water over him. No response. She refilled the bucket and dumped its contents over his face. He moaned.

She repeated the process. Another moan as he struggled to open his eyes. He blinked away the saltiness. Coughed. Spluttered. Bridget threw another bucket and Pierre turned his head to the side and groaned. The harsh timber decking scratched his face, and his eyes sprang open. He thrashed his head. His eyes darted. And when he realised the seriousness of his predicament, he began to rock back and forth.

Bridget dropped the bucket and walked to his side. Her identity was perfectly hidden. In her dress rehearsals it had been impossible to identify her as a man or woman. Pierre Rainer would have no clue.

Pierre squirmed; rolled to his side. She tapped her steel-capped boot against his bloodied nose. He flinched and struggled to move away, pushing as far back against the side of the boat as he could. But there was no escape. His lips began to quiver. His face reddened, and his eyes became wide. Bridget picked up a steel bar and delivered short, sharp blows, one after another, to his body. Jab. Prod. Poke. Her strikes became harder, the intensity increasing to match her rage. *God, I hate him!* He deserved everything he got. He had stripped her of her dignity, robbed her of her life.

"Who are you? Why are you doing this?" he screamed. "Stop! Please stop… please let me go!" But she would not.

Fifteen minutes passed and her terrorising continued. She threw water over his struggling body. She kicked and poked. Pierre's howls danced in the breeze and disappeared into the distant waves. His pain was evident, and the screams in her mind were silenced. A calmness washed over her as she dished out his punishment. Looking into his terror-stricken eyes she remained silent. She wondered if he'd seen a similar fear reflected in her eyes when he'd launched his attacks, when he had had her trapped. She wanted him to experience the dreaded unknown. She wanted him to feel the trauma and unpredictability of the situation. He had abused, harassed, threatened, and assaulted her. She recalled how in one instance Pierre had lunged forward and groped her breasts. She screamed and pushed him away. Pierre laughed, clutched his groin, thrust his hips, and then released a loud moan. Members of staff watched and giggled. When asked by management no one acknowledged the incident. Pierre claimed he had tripped, said it was a dreadful accident. Bridget knew better. His action was deliberate. It was not the first time he had placed his hands on her and it would not be the last. Her stomach churned as her anger grew.

His whimpering began to get on her nerves. She had greeted his pleas with silence. Time to take her attack up another notch. She had heard enough and seen enough. She was wet and cold. Crystal salt covered her body. No doubt Pierre was traumatised beyond anything he could imagine, but for Bridget things were far from over. She needed to silence his pleas for mercy. She was sick of his bellowing.

She grabbed the bottom of the balaclava and yanked it up and over her face. Pierre flinched. What little colour he had fled, almost as if he had come face to face with the grim reaper. He stared. His mouth dropped open. For a moment he froze. Then his body began to shake violently, as he *finally* grasped the gravity of the situation. His attacker was no longer unknown. His life flashed before him. Utter hopelessness filled his body. Bridget was a crazy bitch, a woman possessed. Tears streamed down his face. The air appeared cold and thick. His loud whimpering echoed around them.

"You…" It was more a whisper. "It's you…"

"Shut up! Shut the fuck up!"

Pierre froze, then began to sob. He was exactly where she needed him to be. Defenceless.

"You know I picked this place especially for you. It's so hard for me to find joy these days. You stole that from me, *Pierre.* The way you twisted everyone around your fat little fingers for your own amusement. You *disgust* me," Bridget said, leaning forward. "You destroyed my life, my sense of trust. I carry around so much guilt and shame because I couldn't stop you. I ask myself everyday why… why did I allow you to do that to me?" She paused, took a deep breath and clenched her hands. She stared then spat. "You know what I'm talking about. You know every gory little detail. You know what you did. You spun and contorted everything so you would come out smelling like roses. You claimed to be the protector of the innocent. You claimed you stood up for the simple worker and that I picked on you due to your position as the Union Delegate. They were all lies. You were a master manipulator but you will manipulate no more."

Bridget seethed. Water lashed the deck. Anger filled the air. The clouds turned black. She grasped his shoulder as his tears glistened, and she spat her words at him.

"What you did ruined my life. I wanted to go to sleep and not wake up. Do you realise each day I asked myself why? Why would someone bully me? Why didn't you stop when you saw the pain you were inflicting? How could anyone find joy in ruining someone else's life?" She delivered a stinging slap. "You made my life hell. I felt as if I was sinking in quicksand. Tell me… tell me why. I want to know why," she screamed. She glared down at him, and in his eyes she saw a reflection of fear. Did he recall seeing the same in her eyes when he had her pinned against the wall? His finger prodding into her chest, his voice loud and threatening?

"Why?" she screamed.

"I don't know," Pierre said, as he burst into tears. Turning his head away, his body shook.

Bridget felt no pity. He deserved no sympathy. "I'll tell you why. Because you are a good for nothing *bastard* that felt empowered by someone else's suffering, a narcissistic prick who thought it possible to destroy another." She slapped him again, bringing his attention back to her. "The only thing you didn't anticipate was my resilience. You see, you did knock me down and yes it has been years but I'm back now, stronger than ever. I'm invigorated. *Alive*." She leaned in close. "In control. I'm patient, and I know how to derive joy from the simple things. You see, it's the simple things in life that matter, and while I cannot stop the waves of emotions I've experienced, I can stop *you*." Bridget turned her back on him and walked to the back of the boat. When she glanced back at him, he was staring at the large pile of chain coiled on the deck between where he lay and she stood. She watched as his gaze travelled the length of chain, his eyes widening when they came to rest on the large grey block. The block moved slowly as she pushed, and Pierre struggled to free his hands. A scream bursting free when he realised his efforts were in vain. Bridget ignored him. A splash. The boat rocked. Bridget stood and faced Pierre. She smiled. The coiled chain sprang into motion, and Pierre released a deathly scream. The clanging of metal increased in intensity. Knocking, vibrating, rattling.

Clack, clack, clack, clack, clack, clack, clack.

Pierre's eyes bulged. His face now a glowing red beacon. He screamed. The veins in his forehead protruded. He began trashing, trying to cling to anything that would prevent him being pulled into the icy waters.

"Stop it!" he bellowed. "God please, stop it… I beg you!"

Clack, clack, clack, clack, clack, clack, clack.

"No, this is for all I suffered."

"Please…" he begged.

"No," Bridget snapped. She smiled, as she watched his terror. His screams music to her ears.

Clack, clack, clack, clack, clack, clack, clack.

Looking down she stared at the chain. The pile that had once stood at a height just below her knees was now half way down her shin. A feeling of disappointment overwhelmed her. She hadn't anticipated it would unwind so quickly. She wanted his suffering to be slow. Pierre released more howls.

She smiled. It was a forced habit. She had been told so many times that the best thing to do was to smile so he would not know he affected her. She certainly didn't want him thinking she was in any way disappointed, not at this late stage. Pierre continued thrashing and screaming and abusing.

"You fucken crazy cunt! I should have gotten rid of you when I had the chance," he spat.

Standing in front of him she showed no fear, his words meant nothing. He meant nothing.

Clack, clack, clack, clack, clack, clack, clack.

A couple more minutes and her fun would be over. *Thank God I had decided to travel out so deep in the ocean.*

Resting against the side of the boat, she placed her hands on her hips and grinned. She wanted him to see her face. She wanted him to know exactly who she was. She wanted him to know who was responsible for his suffering. She began to laugh. This would be something she would never forget. Revenge was fantastic!

Clack, clack, clack, clack, clack, clack, clack.

"Not long now," she sang out. "A couple more metres!"

"Please!" he screeched.

She stared at him, expressionless. *When you react, you give other people the power.* There was no way she would react to his pleas. He was powerless. His cries meant nothing.

Whack!

The boat heaved. Bridget was tossed to the right and stumbled to maintain her footing. The chain stopped moving. All was silent. While her focus had been on Pierre, the swell had gained momentum. She feared the powerful waves might be enough to capsize her boat. Clouds swirled above. The air became thick with salt. The wind carried pelting rain that lashed her face. Angry waves soaked the deck. *Control. Stay in control.*

"Ha! I got you," she laughed.

Pierre burst into tears. He was bleeding, terrified and

gasping for breath. "You bitch! You fucken crazy bitch! You're going to go to gaol," he yelled.

His words infuriated her. She launched her left foot into his chest; she wanted nothing more than for him to be silenced. "No, I'm not. The way I see it, you have two choices and I have one pair of bolt cutters." The smile she gave him was cold. "You can continue to threaten me and I will cut the link that holds you to the boat or you WILL keep your mouth shut and I may let you live." She shrugged. "Your choice. You see I know where you live. I know what you eat. I know where you drink and what you drink. I know where your parents live. I know who your partner is. Judy is having a great time in Newcastle." She crouched, smiled again. "It would be horrible if any of them had an accident. I know you would feel terrible, maybe even responsible if something were to happen." He flinched at that. "You see I know everything about you and I can get to you or anyone that you know, wherever and whenever I like." She tilted her head as she stared at him. "And if you do make me come back, I will make your loved ones a stepping stone. I will make them bleed and cry and scream out your name. I will make you watch, then I will make them watch as I kill you. But that's not the best part…" She chuckled. "If you think you're in pain now, you are sadly mistaken… one wrong move from you and I will send you straight to *hell*."

"Please, not my family… Please, I won't say anything. You have my word, I promise," he cried.

"I know you won't… you see I know more than you think. I know you've been screwing around behind Judy's back. I know you've been taking money from the work-betting club and that's just the start. I've been watching you, and like I said I can get you whenever I like." She smirked. "I got you before and I will do it again. And even if you were to dare open your mouth and say something then it will be my word against yours, except this time I have an alibi and you have *nothing*. You see, this time I have the power and I have nothing to lose."

"I won't tell a soul. You have my word… I promise you," he croaked, as he shook his head. His voice was hoarse and quavering. He was defeated. He was broken.

Bridget nodded. "Take this as your warning and thank your lucky stars I'm in a good mood."

Walking to the front of the boat Bridget grabbed the side rail. Large waves surged towards them. Strong howling winds delivered more pelting rain. Pierre watched her every move. His loud panting danced in the breeze and disappeared into the dark sky. The temperature had dropped. Bridget knew she had to get out of there before waves tipped them over. She picked up her bolt cutters. Pierre pleaded to be freed. He begged for a drink. His voice was cracked. He was beaten.

Bridget started the engine. She turned on the winch to retrieve the anchor. She placed the bolt cutters on her seat and shut her eyes relishing her power, then took a deep breath and let it out. Opening her eyes, she picked up a bottle of water, and cracked the seal. Pierre watched her every move. "This water?" she asked. She smiled then placed the bottle to her mouth.

Gulp, gulp, gulp.

Planting her elbow on the steering wheel, she stretched her arm down, pulled her hand back, and flicked her wrist. Water poured from the bottle until it was empty. Bridget laughed.

"Oh no, seems I've had an accident. Isn't that what you used to call them? *Accidents.*"

Pierre glared without comment. Bridget refused to look away. Silence. Moments passed. Finally, he blinked and looked at her with sheepish eyes. She threw him a bottle. He opened the lid with his mouth and sculled the contents. Bridget stared. Smiled. She pulled back the throttle and headed parallel to the coastline. The bow of the boat crashed through the waves. Her body jolted as she gripped the wheel.

She would have to zigzag her way back to the heads so the swell wouldn't tip them over and swallow them. She needed to focus on her safety. Pierre would soon be asleep. *What a fool.* The Mogadon-spiked water would have him sleeping by the time she made her way back to the boat ramp. She would cover his body beneath a tarp. She would take him back to his home. She would dump his body on his back lawn. No one would see him there. When he woke he would be battered and bruised. He would be fearful. He would remember what she had done, but he would have no proof. He'd been outplayed, outsmarted, and he would know she could strike at any moment. She was a crazy bitch, capable of anything – that's what he'd said. He would remain silent. He would fear her reprisals. How could he admit to being overpowered by a woman? He was a man. He would be considered a joke.

Bridget hoped beyond hope he would keep his mouth shut.

CHAPTER TWENTY

Bridget dashed into Daniel's office at 10am without responding to his greetings. Her eyes were red and puffy. Her face flushed. It was clear she had been crying. She looked like a nervous wreck. Her clothes were crumpled. Her hair was a mess. Daniel locked the door behind her then turned on both his desk lamp and the tripod lamp. He pulled the curtains closed as she took her familiar corner chair. He retrieved some tissues and lent against his desk.

"What's happened?" he asked, as he passed her the tissues. "You haven't had another run in with Zack have you?"

Bridget shook her head. She closed her eyes and lowered her face.

"Bridget… talk to me, that's why I am here. You need to talk to me."

"Listen," she suddenly blurted. "There's something I need to tell you." She took a shaky breath. "Something's happened."

"You can tell me anything," he said, as he lent forward and grabbed her hand.

"I did it!" she said, tears now streaming down her face. Her body shook, as she struggled to catch her breath. Daniel's eyebrows furrowed as he squeezed her hand.

"What have you done?" he asked, his voice raised.

"I got Pierre Rainer… I got him."

"Oh no, please tell me you didn't take it too far."

"Too far? What's too far for that bastard," Bridget snapped. "I used some of those Mogadon tablets from your cabin. I drugged him, I beat him and I took him to the ocean. I scared the crap out of him." She released a nervous laugh, as more tears streamed down her face.

"Please tell me you didn't kill him," Daniel begged.

Bridget shook her head, "No I didn't kill him, but now I'm starting to doubt what I did. This revenge thing has left a bitter taste in my mouth. I'm struggling, Daniel. Don't get me wrong… I loved paying them back. They got everything they deserved. But I'm scared of retaliation. What happens if they talk? What happens if Samuel Easton and Arthur Fuller believe I was behind what happened to them?" Fear shook her voice and started to cascade through her body, and he squeezed her hand. "All it takes is for Pierre to open his big mouth and… that's it. Every day I wonder what they're doing. Have they put two and two together? Every day I pray they'll just leave me in peace." Those dark eyes of hers peered up into his. "What they did has haunted me for years. It would be so wonderful to hear they'd been wiped from existence. Every day I hope Pierre will keep his promise to remain silent. But can I trust him? Why should I trust him?" She shook her head. "I'm consumed by doubt. Maybe I should have just pushed him overboard. His body was chained. The concrete block would have sent him to a watery grave. Watery grave." Bridget repeated then laughed. "Makes him sound like he's the fucken Titanic." Daniel watched as Bridget picked at her nails, it was a nervous habit she was trying to break. "Maybe that's where he belongs, at the bottom of the ocean. He'd never have been found. Oh shit what have I done?"

She placed her hands over her face, "Oh fuck, maybe I should have killed him. I could have lived with that. It's the unknown that's killing me." She sobbed, as she rose from her chair and began pacing around the room.

Daniel stepped towards her, grabbed her and pulled her

to him. He wrapped his arms around her, and she burst into tears. "Shhh… it's going to okay." Daniel paused, his voice softening. "I hear what you're saying but you don't have to worry. You're not alone. I'm here for you now. We're going to get through this together. They won't hurt you. I won't let them hurt you." He held her back a little, making her look into his eyes when he spoke, so she could see the truth in his words. "I'll protect you. I promise."

He reached up and wiped away her tears. The last thing he wanted was for her to feel helpless or isolated. Her tear-stained cheeks and bloodshot eyes, made his heart ache. She wrapped her arms around him, and she embraced his warmth. She cherished his words. She wanted to believe he was right Daniel could feel her heart breaking as she clung to him. He held her tight and let the torrent of her tears soak his shirt. She needed to release her pain and frustration. She needed to know he would remain by her side, that he'd never abandon her.

She finally stepped back and gazed into his eyes. Her brow furrowed as she attempted to smile. She nodded. "I need to get out of here. I need to get away. I have to go away. You didn't see the fire in his eyes. I know he said he wouldn't tell, but I can't stop thinking about his eyes." Her trembling started again; he wasn't sure she was aware of it. "The hate was so piercing. I feel like I'm suffocating, Daniel. I want it all to stop. I need it to stop. I need to get away, to breathe without restriction, to live without constantly looking over my shoulder." She sniffed, wiped at her eyes. "Maybe I could to go to the police… if I confess to what I've done, explain why I did it, then maybe just maybe they will understand. They will…"

"They will what?" He shook his head at her. "I'm not going to let you destroy your life. No way. You're worth so much more than that. You've come so far and I won't let you do it. I won't let them destroy you." He took a breath; it was time to admit what he'd been denying for so long. "I love you Bridget, I love you…" Daniel pulled her close.

"Go away if you feel you need to, but wait until next week," he whispered against her ear. "Come to my cabin for the weekend first. We need to talk, Bridget. I need to spend time with you. I want to say things I can't say here. Hilary likes to eavesdrop sometimes. Please…"

Bridget looked deep into Daniel's eyes. She looked like she was calculating the depths of something inside, making sure the pieces fit.

"I will," she said. "I'll come away with you for the weekend but then I am out of here."

"Okay…" he said with a smile. "We'll spend time together. We'll talk where no one will overhear, and then you'll go away," he said, nodding in agreement with her plan. "Now I want you to go home. I want you to run yourself a nice bath and soak in the warm water and relax. Try not to worry, just think of your breath and the warm water. Inhale the stillness; listen to your breath. Remember my mindfulness instructions." He tilted her chin towards him. "It's going to be okay. It's all going to work out. Relax for the week. They can't harm you, and I'm a phone call away." He smiled at her. "I'll pick you up Friday afternoon. It's all going to work out okay."

CHAPTER TWENTY-ONE

Samuel Easton, Arthur Fuller, and Pierre Rainer were spooked. They needed to regroup. Their annual camping trip booked for the following week couldn't have arrived at a better time. For the past eleven years they had escaped for one week of total seclusion. It was a time for camping, fishing, eating and drinking. Partners were not permitted, and what happened during their time together remained between the three.

Pierre had turned up to work Monday morning sporting a broken nose. His right eye was a black slit that sat out like a golf ball. He told his co-workers he had stumbled in his garden while building a new rockery. No one questioned him, but Samuel and Arthur knew better. Their suspicions were confirmed by the glaring look in his eyes when they confronted him.

Bridget would pay.

"One lone bitch won't stand a chance against a three pronged attacked," Pierre snarled. "We got rid of her before. This time we will do it permanently."

"She made me a laughingstock," Samuel hissed. "My daughter found it amusing. How will I ever live it down? I had to top soil my complete lawn to hide her nasty work."

"What about me?" Arthur said, "Jill won't even talk to me. I'm a few years away from retirement and I'm going to end up with nothing. Adolf Titler must pay. That bitch has ruined my life."

"Oh, she'll pay," Pierre snarled. "She thinks she's so smart. Says she can get us whenever or wherever she likes. By the time I'm finished with her, she'll wish she never lived. Look at my face," Pierre said then pulled up the sleeves of his jacket. "Look at my bloody wrists, the bitch had me bound and gagged. She had me drugged and shackled." He balled his hands into fists. "She took me out into the middle of the bloody ocean and was going to kill me. She threatened my family. She has no regard for anyone. She's a crazy cunt. Oh, she'll pay all right. If it's the last thing I do, I'll make her pay." His face reddened with rage. "We'll take next week to plan, and we'll strike as soon as we come back. Bridget Tilner will be no more."

"Why wait?" Samuel asked. "We could hit her tonight. We could drive around and smash her windows with rocks. We could egg her car. Put prawns in her exhaust pipe. We could pour sugar in her fuel tank – that would stuff her up."

"No, no… I have a better idea," said Arthur. "We could pour brake fluid over her car and watch the paint strip away. Remember we did that to Andie Longmore? Remember how he cried?" Arthur laughed, as the others chuckled and smiled.

"No… I want this bitch gone," Pierre snapped, "I want her gone for good. We need to wait. We need to plan. We need to get this right. But for now, we need to go about our business as if nothing's happening. No one must suspect a thing, at least not her. We have to take her seriously. She may be watching us. We need to continue with our lives, work as we would normally work and when we're away next week, we'll have the time and space, the privacy to organise how we can get rid of her once and for all."

Samuel and Arthur nodded in agreement. Pierre always had the final say. Arguing would get them nowhere. The three shook hands. Their word was their bond.

CHAPTER TWENTY-TWO

Arriving at the cabin, Bridget felt the weight of the world release from her shoulders. She would spend the next two days with Daniel. On Monday, she was booked to fly to Melbourne. Daniel had offered to drive her to the airport. Sitting in the sun she stared off into nothingness. She appeared deep in thought.

Daniel smiled and waved his hand in front of her face. "Earth to Bridget, Earth to Bridget, come in Bridget," he laughed. "What are you thinking?"

"Have you ever thought about the small things in life? How the most minuscule thing could change everything? Maybe it already has," she said. "That delay you may have experienced in traffic, the person who pushed in front of a queue. Were their actions of rushing past only making death arrive sooner?"

Daniel laughed, "Oh my, you are such a worry wart. Death comes to everyone. Thinking about it won't make it arrive any sooner or later. You need to focus on the positives, Bridget."

"I know, I know," she said with a sigh. "I just can't help thinking about things. You have to believe me when I say I am trying. I just keep on worrying about those three. What if they put two and two together? What I if they come after me. What if they find the clothes I was wearing?"

"You kept the clothes? Why didn't you throw them away?"

Daniel asked, concern etching his features.

"I just hid them. I didn't have time. I stashed them under my house where I put the lawn mower. I didn't think anyone would find them there. But now that I'm going away… What happens if someone goes there and finds them?"

"They won't. Tell me, has anyone ever been where you store your lawn mower?"

"No, well only Zack," Bridget said. "Oh shit, what happens if Zack goes snooping while I'm away? What happens if he finds the clothes?"

"He won't. You have to stop torturing yourself with all these wild thoughts," Daniel said, closing his hand over hers.

"Maybe I shouldn't have done any of it," she said then chuckled. "But I have to say it felt so good."

Daniel laughed with her. "I love it when you smile, you don't do it enough."

Bridget could tell he was glad she'd agreed to come to the cabin with him. It was clear he wanted to get closer to her – he'd said he loved her.

She thought about the passing looks he had given her over the years. She had caught his staring eyes while in therapy. The way he leant forward when she spoke. His words teased. Their innocent conversations turned naughty. Daniel had a far-away look in his eyes, but a soft smile played about his lips. Was he thinking about them taking another step in their relationship? Was he as nervous as she? His fingers gently touched her face, and he leaned forward until his lips met hers.

"I want you," she murmured.

Her hands moved lightly around his nape.

Daniel stroked her hair; gently brushed at the stray strands that covered her face as he gently kissed her. He pulled back gently and scanned her face, back and forth like he was reading a book.

"We need to talk," he said quietly.

Bridget frowned. "Talk…" she said as her hands dropped to her side. She turned away and Daniel pulled her back into him.

"Bridget, please we need to talk. You know I can't keep seeing you, if I'm to continue as your therapist. I don't know about you, but I can't deny the feelings I have for you. I've watched you for years. Admired you for years. I kept my distance because you had Zack… but now I don't want to keep my distance. I am falling for you, Bridget. I think I've loved you from the first moment I saw you. But we can't do this… we can't do this while I am your psychiatrist."

Bridget released a loud sigh then dropped her face. She freed herself from Daniel's hold and looked directly into his eyes. She knew he meant every word. "Find me one then," she snapped. "Find me a new psychiatrist. I'm sick of living like this. I want to move forward. I want to move forward with you, Daniel. I'm not going to let those three bastards ruin my plans. Promise me… promise me you'll do it."

Daniel nodded, "I will… I promise. I'm here for you, Bridget. You don't have to worry about those bastards. They have no proof you've done anything. They'll get what they deserve, and I'll find you a new therapist. I want you more than anything, but I cannot cross that line. Not yet."

Bridget lent forward and whispered in his ear, "I know you want what's best for me. I know you want what's best for us. I trust you'll never let me down and I'll never let you down either." Bridget's hand wandered to his thigh as she kissed him.

The remainder of the weekend was spent enjoying each other's company. Neither spoke about their close encounter, and both continued with the playful teasing, close encounters, and penetrating gazes. They knew what they wanted. They knew they had restrictions that required resolving before they could move forward. Nothing would jeopardise what they desired.

Daniel drove Bridget to the airport. Removing her luggage from his car, he placed it on the footpath then looked into her eyes, smiled, and wrapped his arms around her. Bridget pulled him close. He could feel the warmth of her embrace; again, his loins were on fire. Bridget closed her eyes. Daniel inhaled her sweet scent, and pulled her even closer. He felt a tingling sensation down below. There was no denying the spark. They kissed. They hugged. Daniel promised to do as she had asked. They would reunite when she returned. Nothing would ever come between them.

CHAPTER TWENTY-THREE

Sitting around the crackling campfire, the three ate and drank as they watched the flames flicker. Stars sparkled in the blackness that enveloped the sky. A half-moon sat overhead surrounded by a misty ring of clouds. Three tents had been erected in a semi-circle skirting the fire. Firewood was stacked around the outer rim of the fire pit, bordered with a mix of large and small bush rocks. Three logs had been pulled from the dense bushland. They were positioned as stools so the three could gather around the warmth. The day had been a great success. Tonight they ate fresh fish. Their voices echoed out into the darkness of the dense bushland that surrounded them. They were alone. It was a time to plan their attack.

Pierre looked at his friends, wondering if they could be trusted. They'd covered for one another before but they'd never contemplated murder. Would they follow through with their silence? Arthur had lost everything. His wife had left him. He appeared to have nothing left to lose. But Samuel was another story. He had a beautiful wife and daughter. Would he risk his freedom? Pierre stared at Samuel, as the man picked up the remains of his fish bones and threw them into the fire.

"We need to work out our plan," Pierre said. "I need to know you'll both go through with what we decide. The bitch must pay, but I have to be sure you'll both keep your mouths shut."

"Of course we will," Arthur said. "That whore ruined my life. I want her dead just as much as you."

Samuel looked across the fire at Pierre. He hesitated.

"Samuel," Pierre snapped. "What about you? Can we count on you when the time comes?"

"Jesus Christ, what type of question is that? Of course you can," Samuel said as he threw his beer can into the fire. Seemed he was annoyed Pierre doubted his loyalty.

"There's no need to jump down my throat. It's a question I had to ask for an answer I needed to hear." He stared hard at Samuel. "There can be no second-guessing. There'll be no turning back. What we decide here *must* stay between the three of us. We have to work together, and promise that no matter what, we'll never discuss what we did." He shifted his gaze between his two friends. "We have to kill her before she kills us, and when we do, we have to be certain our secret goes to our graves with us."

Samuel and Arthur nodded in agreement. Samuel grabbed another beer from his esky. "I'll drink to that," he cheered, as he threw fresh beers to the others.

Pierre stared at him then glanced towards Arthur. He hated Bridget. He wanted nothing more than to see her dead. The last thing he wanted was for one of his so called friends to stuff up his plans. He wondered if he should have just kept his mouth shut. Maybe getting them involved had been a mistake. He wanted to ask them again, wanted to double-check their loyalty and commitment but thought better of it. He had to believe in their word. A man's word was his bond, his father had always told him. Pierre had to be confident, and they had covered for one another in the past.

Cracking open his can, Pierre guzzled his beer and pushed to his feet. He paced around the fire, picked up a log and threw it onto the flames, watching as embers flew. The timber popped and crackled. Smoke filled the air and sparks danced high. An amber glow lit their campsite and made shadows dance over their surrounds.

"We need to attack her in her home," Pierre said, as he rubbed a hand over his face then through his hair. "At night. We'll attack at night while she's sleeping. I know her boyfriend's left her. She'll be alone." He grinned, then burped loudly. "She won't know what hit her."

"When?" Samuel asked.

"As soon as we get back. We can't let another minute pass."

Samuel looked down into the fire and tossed a small branch into the flames, "How will we get inside?"

"I know she still goes to see a shrink," Pierre said. "Been going to him for years. Seen her dash into his office. Every appointment is always in the morning at the same time. All we have to do is find out when her next appointment is, and when she leaves her house, we break in. We can leave a window unlocked. She won't suspect a thing. Then when she's sleeping, we'll attack."

Samuel shivered and gulped down his beer as reality struck. Pierre was serious. There would be no turning back.

CHAPTER TWENTY-FOUR

Crouched behind the bushes my heart raced. Palms clammy, sweat trickled from under my armpits. The pressure was on. This was the moment I'd been waiting for. Fear of being spotted kept me still and alert. Samuel Easton, Arthur Fuller and Pierre Rainer sat drinking around their campfire. The three became more intoxicated as the minutes passed. Darkness, we were all surrounded by darkness. Scattered beer cans covered the ground. It would soon be time to strike. No way could they continue. Bullying bastards. They would destroy no more. No mercy would be given.

Pierre stood and stretched, his gaze moving over my hiding spot. He threw his discarded beer can. It struck the nearby tree trunk and fell within reach. Pierre's head tilted, hands raised to his forehead as he stared. He took a few steps forward. Closer. Branches and twigs cracked beneath his feet. He paused. *One wrong move…*

He took another step forward. Paused again as he stared.

"Oi, Pierre what ya doin'?" Arthur slurred his words. "Why don't you fetch us another drink while you're up."

Pierre glanced back over his shoulder. "I thought I saw something," he said, rubbing his eyes.

"Oh no! Watch out for the boogeyman," Samuel laughed.

"I'll give you fucken boogeyman. Get your own fucken drink," Pierre snapped.

"Oh come on, lighten up…" said Samuel, laughing again. "I was only joking. Why don't you grab that bottle?"

"What bottle?" Pierre asked, turning back to the fire.

A sigh of relief. *Patience.*

"You said some guy gave it to you the other night when you were leaving the pub, some old guy you've known for years."

"Oh that bottle." Pierre nodded, "Old Billy Tappet gave it to me, said someone gave it to him and we should take it with us."

"Well go on then, what are you waiting for? I think we need to drink a toast to our up and coming success." Arthur chuckled, "I can't wait to see the look in that bitch's eyes when she sees us."

Pierre shook his head and smiled. "What… so now you want to do the honours?"

"Why not? She's ruined my life. Jill won't even talk to me. I've lost *everything*. I want that bitch to see my face when she struggles for her final breath," he said, spittle flying from his lips.

"What you want and what you get are two very different fucken things," Pierre snarled. "Look what she has done to me. She nearly killed me! She threatened my *family*. Says she can get me whenever she fucken likes!" He balled his hands into fists. "I'll show her who'll get fucken who." He stomped over to the fire. "I want to wrap my hands around her bloody throat and squeeze as tight as I can. I want to stare into her eyes. Feel her struggle beneath me. I want to spit in her face, then snap her fucking neck." Pierre clenched his hands in front of his stomach and motioned a snapping action.

***

Samuel sat quietly, listening and watching his friends, his expression pensive. Their words were full of hate. He wondered if it was the alcohol talking. He wanted Bridget to pay for her actions but murder, he wasn't sure if he was capable of murdering anyone. What would happen if they got caught? He would lose his family. He would lose his freedom. His daughter already thought he was a joke. How would she handle a father being convicted of murder? To retaliate against someone who caused pain was one thing, but murder? Samuel hoped the light of day would deliver sense. For now he just needed another drink, something stronger than beer.

"A little less talk and a bit more action," Samuel laughed nervously. "Weren't you going to get us that drink?"

Pierre smiled and nodded "Oh so I was," he replied enthusiastically, turned and kicked an empty beer can then stumbled towards his tent. He unzipped the flap and dove inside. The campsite fell silent. A few minutes later Pierre emerged with a bottle that held a dark amber liquid.

"Let's drink to our success," he cheered, as he raised the bottle above his head. "Grab me those mugs," he demanded, pointing towards their supplies next to the esky.

Arthur scurried over and retrieved three mugs as instructed. He smiled as he passed them out. Pierre poured for all three, spilling some of the drink onto the ground before throwing the empty bottle into the fire.

He held his mug at waist height. "I'd like to propose a toast…" he said, looking towards his mates and smiling. "To friends, and to the death of Bridget Tilner. May she rot in hell!" He cheered, as he raised his mug.

Samuel and Arthur repeated his words. All three sculled the contents of their mugs. Samuel went to the esky and retrieved another three beers, and the men sat around the fire watching the flames.

Pierre studied his friends' faces. Was that determination in his eyes? Set, no doubt on the killing. Would he be able to trust the other two to keep their mouths shut? What would he do if they dared to cross him? Would they become an enemy?

Samuel met Pierre's gaze, but couldn't hold it, looking away as he poked at the fire. Contemplation sat on Samuel's face. What doubts did he hold? Murder seemed to weigh heavy on him. If so, where would he stand if he did not comply with their demands? He questioned whether his big burly mate would be capable of murder. He had seen first hand how others had suffered at his hands. He had never dared to cross Pierre. Too many people had crumbled beneath his power. But murder?

***

Arthur appeared half-asleep. His face was ashen, his cheeks drawn. All his earlier talk of smothering someone seemed unlikely, but who knew? The man had had heart surgery, and was half the size of his friend, Pierre.

Arthur sat smiling into his drink. His heavy eyes flickered. Darkness met his exhaustion. The crackling flames had been mesmerising. A day fishing in the sun with hours of drinking had been taxing. He thought of the mateship he shared with his friends. His mates were his life. Besides their friendship he had nothing. He closed his eyes. He soaked up the warmth from the flames. He was content. He gently lowered his can next to his side and placed it on the ground. He wriggled around and adjusted his position. The log behind comfortably supported him. His breath became shallow. He would soon be asleep.

All three would never make it to their tents.

CHAPTER TWENTY-FIVE

Along the tree-lined streets of Sydney, nothing much had changed except three co-workers were mysteriously missing. Samuel Easton, Arthur Fuller and Pierre Rainer were rostered to commence their shift at 8am, and all three had failed to show. Not even a phone call by way of explanation.

Veronica Easton was in a flap. She hadn't managed any sleep. Nor had she been able to contact her husband. He'd been due home yesterday afternoon, and she'd even baked his favourite dinner – meatloaf with mashed potatoes and peas plus bread and butter pudding. She'd kept his plate warm, just as he liked, and she had waited patiently.

He never showed.

His dinner now sat covered in the fridge. A niggling feeling told her something was wrong. Very wrong. She'd not seen or heard from Samuel since he left with his two mates over a week ago. Pierre Rainer and Arthur Fuller had picked him up before sunrise the previous Saturday. Veronica had been in bed when they arrived. She'd heard their voices, heard them mention fishing, but Samuel hadn't told her where they were heading. He'd left without as much as a kiss on the cheek. *They could be anywhere.* Tears fell as she looked at her watch, then glanced out the front window. It was too early to contact the police to file a missing person's report. She prayed he was safe and well. She'd not heard of any major traffic accidents.

She again checked that the telephone was working. How could her beloved husband just vanish? Why hadn't he called to tell her what was happening?

Sharon Easton thanked the gods for her father's disappearance. She was glad he was missing. He was a thorn in her side. Contrary to his belief, the male population was not the superior race. The voices and views of women were not something to be ignored. *I hope he never comes back.* She didn't care where he was. Besides her mother's worrying cries, her home was peaceful for once. Sharon loved this time of year. She looked forward to her father's time away with his mates. It was one week of freedom. Time without him in the family home delivered harmony, cooperation and peace. She could use the bathroom when she chose. She didn't have to endure her father's demands. Respect. Her home possessed respect. And the toilet seat was never left up. Looking at her mother she could see the worry in her eyes, could feel her concern, and hear the nervousness in her trembling voice.

"It's going to be okay," Sharon told her mother. "They've probably just drunk too much, maybe they've broken down or have a flat tyre. He'll be home soon enough," she said, as she wrapped her arm around her mother.

Veronica shrugged away her daughter's arm and paced the lounge room. She ran to the front window when she heard a car. "I should have insisted he tell me where they were going," she said, as she shook her head.

"He wouldn't have told you, it was secret-squirrel business, the private man's club," Sharon scoffed.

"That's enough! Can't you see I have enough to worry about than to listen to your smart comments?"

"Well I'm sure you would've told dad where you were going. I have to say where I'm going all the time," Sharon snapped. "I don't see why there's one rule for us and another for him," Sharon said, as she rolled her eyes and looked towards the ceiling.

"I said that is enough," Veronica said sharply, then burst into tears.

Her mother was a loyal wife who never questioned her husband.

***

Judy Coleman looked out the rear window, past the flowers in the garden and towards the garage. Her eyes were blurry and her head was thumping. She had a massive hangover. She'd had a big weekend with her girlfriends and was relieved to have a rostered day off work. She had no memory of arriving home last night. She'd not made it to bed; instead she spent the night on the lounge. When she finally staggered to the bedroom, the bed was made and she collapsed on top of it. She placed her hands over her head and asked herself why she had drunk so much. She frowned. Something hadn't seemed right when she looked out into the backyard. What had she seen? Her brow furrowed further. Something sticking out from behind the garage. In her state, she hadn't been able to work out what it was. She closed her eyes. She couldn't be bothered getting up. She needed sleep.

***

Jill Fuller received a telephone call from Sally Pascoe at Wolf Industries during her morning tea break. Sally had been trying to contact Arthur on his mobile phone but there was no answer. She'd made several attempts, and the only response was an automated message stating his telephone may have been switched off or out of range. The same message she'd received when she'd attempted to contact Samuel Easton and Pierre Rainer.

"Good morning Jill," Sally said. "Sorry to bother you, but

I was wondering if you have seen Arthur. He was due to come back to work today but he hasn't shown. Samuel Easton and Pierre Rainer are also missing."

Sally heard a cackling noise, she wondered if she had dialled the correct number. "Hello Jill, is that you?"

"Yes it's me, and good riddance to the bastard. I would be so lucky if he dropped off the face of the earth." She laughed. "Maybe he's done us all a favour and drowned himself or fallen off a cliff and snapped his neck." Another laugh cut across the line. "You must excuse my harshness, but I used to be his village-idiot wife and doormat. Thank God he's no longer my problem, and it would probably save me significant hassle if he never returned."

The telephone clicked in Sally's ear. It was a response she had anticipated. The poor woman had only recently found out Arthur had been cheating behind her back for years.

Sally Pascoe made another telephone call, this time Veronica Easton answered. She was distraught; many of her words were indecipherable, and she could offer no answers. Veronica insisted someone had to know something. However, the harsh reality struck when Sally informed her Samuel was not the only one missing; all three mates had failed to show for their shift. Veronica burst into tears, and loud wailing filled Sally's ears.

"I'll let you know if I hear anything," Sally said gently. "I'm afraid no one knew where they were going."

Sally terminated the telephone call.

***

Judy's sleep was rudely interrupted by her ringing telephone. Shoving her head beneath her pillow she tried to shut out the noise. It was her day off. Didn't everyone know she wanted a day of peace? The telephone stopped ringing and she breathed a sigh of relief. Then it started again. She pulled her pillow tighter around her pounding head trying to silence the shrill. Whoever it was, they were persistent. On the third call she lunged for her phone.

"What?" she growled.

"Is Pierre there?" the voice asked.

"Who's this?"

"Sally, Sally Pascoe from Wolf Industries."

"Why are you phoning me? Pierre has told you people not to call my phone," she barked as she rubbed her cool hand over her throbbing forehead.

"I wouldn't normally phone you, Judy, but Pierre hasn't shown up for work and I can't reach him."

Judy sat up. She remained silent, thoughts of the backyard intruding. Something appeared out of place. What was it?

"Hang on," she said.

She staggered out of her bedroom, turned right and clung to the wall as she walked through the kitchen. She gazed out the back window. It was still there.

"Hello? Are you there Judy?"

"Hang on, hang on… Hold your fucken horses."

Judy unlocked the back door and walked up the yard. Her hand guarded her face from the bright sun. Her head pounded. In her haste to find out what was behind the garage she forgot to put on shoes and hit a patch of bindi-eye. She jumped and shouted, hopped and cursed. Tiny, sharp needles speared into the soles of Judy's feet. "Ouch, ouch, ah, ah, ouch…fucken bindis," she screamed.

"What the…"

"Judy? Judy?"

"He's here," Judy said.

"Oh, um okay. Can I have a quick word with him please?" Sally asked.

Silence followed. A deathly scream.

"Judy? Judy? Are you there? Judy, what's happening? Is everything alright?"

"I can't find him. He's not here. His car is here. It's full of camping gear. He's not here. I can't find him," a panicked Judy replied.

"Oh okay, well can you get him to give me a call when you see him please."

"You don't understand. He is not here. His car is here. It's full of camping gear. I can't find him."

"Yes, I know… you just told me that, but if you could get him to give me a call when you see him."

"You don't understand… I don't know where he is," Judy cried.

Sally sat listening. All she wanted was for Judy to ask Pierre to telephone. She had understood her the first time when she had said his car was there, but he was not. Her request had been simple. She wondered why she got all the crappy jobs. Why was it people had to babble on the telephone? Why did they feel the need to hang up in her ear? Was it necessary to be rude? The conversation with Judy was going nowhere, and she was just as rude as Pierre – those two were a perfect match. She had better things to do then sit on the telephone. Looking across the office she waved at Marcia from accounts. Sally had had enough.

Just as she was about to hang up she heard Judy's bellowing words. High-pitched screams penetrated her eardrum, like a sickening crazed hyena, "Blood… the car is full of blood! There's blood everywhere. It's over the seats. It's on the dashboard. It's smeared on the window. Oh my God! There's blood everywhere!"

CHAPTER TWENTY-SIX

Samuel Easton began to come to. His mind was fuzzy. His eyelids fluttered. Drool ran down his chin. In the pit of his stomach was an overwhelming sense of dread. His body felt heavy and numb. He couldn't move. He couldn't see. And he couldn't feel his hands or feet. He blinked into absolute darkness. Inhaled a strong odour of rubber. Panic set in. His rapid breathing echoed loudly, and his heart pounded wildly in his chest. *What the fuck? Where am I?* His mind raced a million miles an hour. The last thing he recalled was drinking around the campfire with his mates.

Fear. Samuel was terrified. Silence was thick around him. He blinked furiously, prayed for the light to return to his eyes. Tingling entered his extremities, and his numbness gave way to pain. He began to sob. *Where am I?* Small glimpses of reality bled into his haze. He closed his eyes. Listened. Nothing. A shiver ran down his spine. Cold flooded through him. A strange sound. His eyes sprang open. Soft footsteps shuffled from within the shadows. The silhouette of a person appeared then retreated into the darkness.

"Who are you? What do you want?" Samuel demanded. "Show me your face!" He peered into the shadows, trying to see who hid in the darkened corner of the room.

"I am your worst nightmare, and you are an evil ape. Evil apes must be punished," the voice whispered.

"What are you talking about?"

"Hear no evil," the voice muttered. The floor creaked. His attacker stepped out from the shadows. Samuel stared defiantly. A blinding flash tore into his eyes and he squeezed them closed.

"Why are you doing this?" he bellowed. "Who are you? What do you want?" With caution, he opened his eyes. His attacker was gone. Samuel's gaze darted about but everything was black. Shiny and black. Rippled and folded and smooth and joined. Panic flooded through him again. Short sharp breaths escaped him as he realised he was enclosed within a room lined with black plastic.

Murderers wrapped their victims in plastic. Dead bodies were buried in plastic. *Oh shit… I am going to die.*

"Help! Help! Somebody help me!" His throat burned as screams ripped from him. Someone had to hear him. Where were his mates?

"Help me! Please! Someone… anyone… help!"

No one responded. All was silent. Samuel's efforts appeared hopeless but his vision and mind cleared. He was trapped. Trapped and terrified. A cool breeze crossed his body and he shivered. *Time to take stock.* He could move his neck, and he could lift his head. *Good.* He stared down towards his feet, and his eyes darted over his body as shock hit. He swallowed hard.

Nausea broiled in his gut. He had been violated. Stripped naked, he was spread eagled, wrists and ankles tightly bound to a hard wooden board. He thought of the Vitruvian Man, a drawing by Leonardo da Vinci, a man positioned with his arms and legs outspread. He began to sob. The Vitruvian Man was well proportioned, Samuel was not. Why was he naked? How had he got here? Where was 'here'? Had he been raped? He squeezed his butt cheeks but no pain was evident. *Thank God.*

A loud clanking and rumbling noise erupted outside the

room of black plastic. He focused on the buzzing. It got louder. It was getting closer. *This can't be happening.* He blinked hard hoping he was in a nightmare. "Wake up, wake up, wake up," he begged. His body shook. His heart pounded. Why wouldn't he wake up?

A section of the black plastic moved and an opening appeared. Samuel's heart sank. He was going to die. He was going to be hacked apart. A masked person stood before him. Their identity concealed by a balaclava and large coat. Gloved hands tightly wrapped around the roaring beast. Samuel screamed. His body thrashed as he pulled at his restraints.

"Help! Help! Fuck! Somebody help me!"

His attacker moved closer. Samuel's screaming was drowned out beneath the threatening roar. His thrashing stopped. He froze. His attacker stood near his head. Blasting explosions filled his ears. He peered into the unblinking eyes of his attacker. He tried to work out who it was. *Think!* Minutes passed. It felt like an eternity. His attacker retreated. The roaring stopped and a high pitched ringing filled Samuel's ears. White noise filled his head. He yelled and screamed and yelled and screamed. He could hear nothing except high-pitched ringing. Samuel's world began to close in around him. If he couldn't hear, how would he know if help was on its way? How would he know if his attacker were returning?

Without warning the opening in the plastic thrust apart again. His attacker returned, pointing at him. The balaclava hid their mouth, and Samuel couldn't work out if they were speaking. He began screaming for help again. Surely someone would hear. His attacker bent over and retrieved something from the darkness. A flash burst into Samuel's eyes, followed by another followed then another. Samuel could do nothing to stop the blinding flashes. His throat ached from his yelling. He squeezed his eyes closed when he realised what caused the flashing. *Photos.* Dear God, his attacker was taking photos – one after another, after another. Tears streamed from Samuel's eyes. He felt defiled and violated. What would happen if people saw the photos? How would he ever live it down? He began to sob. His body trembled. His mind whirled. It had to be her. *That fucken bitch.* His eyes sprang open. His attacker had vanished.

"I know it's you," he screamed, "I know you can hear me! I know it's you!"

He closed his eyes. His body trembled. A torrent of tears streamed down his cheeks.

"You fucken bitch! You fucken Adolf Titler bitch," he screamed, as he fought to inhale. His cursing continued as he desperately sucked in large breaths between his sobs. He stopped. Reality hit. If he angered his attacker, he would surely die. If he begged for forgiveness he may be spared.

"I don't want to die," he bellowed, as he began to cough and splutter. "Please, I'm sorry! Please let me go. I won't say a word. Please…" he cried.

A revving vibration filled his body. He screamed as he was thrust into a world of excruciating pain. Sharp metal teeth spun around the edge of a long steel plate. Metal teeth driven by a high-speed chain ate into his thigh. His skin was ripped apart. Warm blood spattered over his body and the black plastic. Rapid spurts sprayed out in time with his pulsating heart. Like some horror movie, the blood went everywhere. So much blood. Then came shards of bone and flesh. Samuel clenched his teeth. He squeezed his eyes closed trying to absorb the pain. Flecks of bone and flesh hit his face. He shut his mouth as he tried not to swallow the taste of his own blood. The cutting stopped. His pain did not. A burning filled his leg. Throbbing pain. He looked down but couldn't tell if his leg had been completely severed. There was too much blood. Vomit sprayed from his mouth. His body became hot and sweaty. His breaths short and sharp. He was going to pass out. His attacker had vanished. Samuel could do nothing, but lie still and pray he would be saved. One minute passed, then one more.

Samuel Easton's eyes became dull and glassy. They fluttered as he struggled to breathe. He could feel his body pulsating. Blood flowed from his open wound. His chest ached. Sorrow overwhelmed him. Images of his wife Veronica swirled in his mind. Did she know he loved her? He wanted her to know he was sorry for everything he'd done wrong. He wished he could go back in time and tell her how he felt, show her the attention she deserved. He wanted to apologise to his daughter, Sharon. He should have been more considerate to her needs. She was a young lady; he should have respected her more. He shouldn't have yelled at her as he had, he should have demanded less of her. He looked towards the door. His breathing became desperate. He was cold. So very cold. His attacker had returned. They stood in the shadows. Between his blinking he saw a large coat. A balaclava covered his attacker's face. Samuel gasped. The room appeared void of oxygen. He stared. His attacker removed their mask.

Samuel met his attacker's eyes. *No... it can't be...* "You," he said, and then his world went dark forever.

CHAPTER TWENTY-SEVEN

Edward Wolf was a rich and powerful businessman. His name was synonymous with Wolf Industries. Initially, he was a man Bridget had admired – successful in business, a family man recognised for his contributions to the community through a variety of philanthropic endeavours. Heck, he was even listed on the *BRW* rich list. Bridget was proud to have her name associated with his. That was until she met the man behind the mask. Edward Wolf hadn't evolved into an accomplished man by being a nice guy. He was ruthless and didn't take kindly to having the darker side of his personality exposed. Bridget found this out within twelve months of being in his employ. She had decided to go to the top with her complaints about bullying and harassment.

"Speak one word of this and I will destroy you," he'd threatened. "I am a powerful man with many friends, and I'll make sure you never work again."

Mr Wolf was nothing more than hypocritical fat bastard. Employees of Wolf Industries sat through compulsory workplace diversity training. Edward Wolf would spruik about the importance of not tolerating shameful behaviour in the workplace, yet, he had made millions on the back of turning a blind eye. He believed he was beyond reproach. To Mr Wolf, nothing was more important than the almighty dollar. Nothing and no one would stop him from making his fortune.

His senior management team consisted of all men, and it was rumoured they would stand around the urinal comparing penis sizes. Their 'I'll scratch your back if you scratch mine' mentality, their sexist behaviour and snide remarks left all the female employees wondering who would be next in the firing line. Most silently believed Mr Wolf simply hired female employees to keep up with appearances within the business world. In essence, he was nothing more than a greedy thug who controlled a team of thugs below him in order to profit. He was an individual who believed in male domination and female submissiveness.

When Bridget Tilner thought of Edward Wolf she felt sick to the stomach. He repulsed her.

When Edward Wolf heard the news about three missing employees he exploded. He was furious – how dare they disappear and affect his ability to do business. Three employees in one branch of his business represented ten percent of that workforce. An absence of ten percent reduced his ability to make money. A workforce running with a declined efficiency could be hit financially.

"Bastards! Inconsiderate bastards," he shouted as he picked up his glass paperweight and hurled it across the room. Glass smashed and shattered over the floor. His secretary flinched and jumped so she would not be hit. "Don't they think about their obligations? What ever happened to loyalty?" he snapped.

"They are missing, Edward," she replied, as she meekly stepped forward and handed him a copy of the Sydney newspaper.

He snatched the paper from her and straightened the page with so much force he nearly tore it. He grunted and cleared his throat then peered over the top of the page. "Who are they?"

"Samuel Easton…"

"Don't know him. Who else?"

"Arthur Fuller…"

"Never heard of him. He means nothing to me."

"Pierre Rainer…"

"What?" His eyebrows rose. "I know that name… he's… he's… he is the bloody Union Delegate." Edward began to laugh. His face reddened, and he removed his glasses and wiped his hands over his face. "Oh wow, oh my," he chuckled. "That bastard has cost me a fortune over the years. Do you know how many people I've had to pay out to keep silent because of him? The disharmony he caused throughout the years has been enormous. I couldn't get rid of him due to the Union." He tried to compose himself. "Oh wow… poor bastard. So you say he is missing?" He raised his eyebrows and pursed his lips. "Well let's hope he stays missing. Contact Human Resources; tell them to send over one individual from three of the surrounding branches. Give it a week, if the guys still haven't shown their ugly heads tell Human Resources to commence interviews for replacements. Oh, and grab me a chocolate thickshake, I think I need a celebratory drink. That will be all."

His secretary stood to the side of his desk taking notes as he spoke; she was used to his outbursts. His glass paperweight was not the first thing she had seen fly across his office. He had been known to throw a chair or two.

CHAPTER TWENTY-EIGHT

Arthur Fuller lay strung out, cold, and trembling. He struggled and strained. His forehead ached and his eyelids pulled. Blackness. He was in a world of complete blackness. No matter how much he strained his eyes, they would not open. It was hopeless. His breath was ragged. His heart pounded and he began to sob. His forehead was a mass of sweat. The pain from the large gash on his right arm was excruciating. Blood seeped through his bandage. He had never seen so much blood. His clothes were covered in the red crimson. He felt weak.

Pierre had been pissed with him. It wasn't his fault. He hadn't asked for the metal to slice his arm. It was in his panic that he had jumped into the car. It was his desperate searching to stop the flow of blood that resulted in him dripping and smearing blood throughout Pierre's car. At the time he hadn't been worried about the mess. His urgency had been in stemming the flow. He feared he had hit an artery. Now his fear had changed. It had grown into its own monster.

A strange noise drifted through his darkness. His heart slammed against his rib cage, and he pissed himself. He had never been more terrified. In the dark, he heard breathing. Creeping footsteps taunted him. He was flat on his back, completely restrained. The footsteps stopped. Whoever it was stood above his head. He could feel warm breath against his forehead. Smell fresh peppermint when they exhaled.

"Shh now," they crooned. "Don't move."

Arthur's lips quivered. His continued to strain to see but no tears could release. "Who are you? What do you want?" he cried, as his sobbing echoed around the room.

"I am your worst nightmare," the voice responded.

Again Arthur had to strain to hear the whisper. "What have you done to me? I can't see! Why can't I see?"

"You are an evil ape. Evil apes must be punished."

Arthur gulped. The voice had moved down to near his waist. He tilted his head to the side, but still he couldn't see.

"See no evil," the voice muttered, as the floor creaked.

Whoever it was continued their taunting. Arthur began sniffing. Attempting to see was useless. His eyelids were stuck. He screamed. His eyelids had been glued shut. "Why are you doing this to me? Why? Tell me why?"

"Because you saw and you did nothing."

Arthur froze. What was this person talking about? Who was it? He needed to get them to talk. He needed to hear the voice clearly. If he knew who it was, then he may be able to bargain his way out. "I'm sorry… I should have done something," he whimpered.

Silence. He couldn't hear them. He couldn't smell them. Where had they gone? Why weren't they talking? He focused on the blackness. "I can make it up to you," he sobbed, as he listened for a clue. Any clue would help.

"No!" One word rang out in the room. One word offered no clues.

Arthur remained still, forcing himself to listen. Soft footsteps. A tug on his left hand. His ring finger was grabbed. Arthur struggled to free his hand.

"Let me go!"

His wrist was held tightly against a hard surface. Struggling was futile. His attacker had all the power. Arthur felt a tugging against his fingernail. A jolt of excruciating pain as his fingernail was ripped free. He screamed.

His attacker laughed.

Arthur cried out in pain as his hand was released. He clenched his hand. Warm blood filled his fist. His finger throbbed. His attacker paced. There was more to come.

"Let's up the ante," the voice whispered in his ear, making him flinch.

Arthur trembled. He was trapped. His attacker snatched his hand again and prised opened his fist. Cold hard steel clamped around the side of his blood-soaked finger. Razor sharpness sliced. Arthur screamed, begging for his attacker to stop. The pressure around his finger increased. Blood dripped.

Snap!

His bone broke beneath the pressure. His finger dropped to the floor.

"You won't be needing that anymore," the voice whispered.

Arthur's screaming clashed with his attacker's laughter. A crushing pain struck the centre of his chest. Agonising pressure. Squeezing. He gasped for air. Broke out in a cold sweat. The veins in his forehead popped. His head thrashed from side to side. His jaw ached and his upper lip became numb. A dull pain began to radiate down his left arm.

"Help me… please help me… I think I'm having a heart attack," he stammered, as he huffed and puffed. Sweat dripped from his forehead. It felt as though a large block had been dropped onto his chest. Why was no one answering? His pain intensified. The burning taste of bile rose in his throat. It felt as though his chest was being ripped open. He gasped for breath then began convulsing. A panicked wheezing sound echoed around the room.

Stillness.

He stopped.
He made no noise.
All was silent.
His struggling arms relaxed.

His panicked facial expression froze.
His mouth remained open.
His eyes were glued shut.
Arthur Fuller was dead.
He would see no more evil.

CHAPTER TWENTY-NINE

Pierre Rainer raised his head, opened his eyes then closed them. He drifted in and out of consciousness. He struggled to inhale. His chin flopped to his chest. Head hammering, it was difficult to focus. His vision was blurred. He was exhausted. Indistinct screams rang in his ears. A large covering of duct tape formed a distinct x pattern across his mouth. It wrapped tightly around his head, pulled at his hair, and circled under his chin. In his weakened state he could do nothing. Five minutes passed, then five more.

His eyelids flickered. He moaned as he tried to work out what was happening. Was he hallucinating? A warm breath danced across his cheek. *Peppermint.* He opened his eyes. A glimpse of a shadowed figure stood near. It disappeared into his cloudiness. His eyelids fell shut. Was he imagining this? Where the hell was he? He had no memory of moving from the campfire.

Time passed, and he battled to put the pieces together. He'd been drinking with his mates. They'd been laughing as they plotted their attack. *No...* Overwhelming horror churned from within. Fear made him sweat. He strained to move; battled to open his eyes. He peered into the darkness. He was alone. Wasn't he?

The sound of his heavy sniffling filled the room. How could he have been so careless and stupid? He should have known she'd be back. He should have known not to trust her. Strapped to a chair, his hands and feet were bound. She must have been following them; they must have been drugged. *Crazy bitch!* She was capable of anything.

He twisted his wrists and strained to free his hands. Ripping and tearing, his panicked pulling tore his skin. The rope ate into his flesh. He could not give in. He'd never give up. Painful cries echoed from the darkness – bellowing pleas for mercy, horrific screams, agonising groans and then silence. A terrible silence.

The thought of what would happen next put a fear in Pierre like nothing else. She could return at any moment. It had to be Bridget Tilner. It had to be her. She'd threatened to kill him. Promised to return if he dared cross her. She was back. He had to break free. There was no way she'd let him live. Not this time.

Focus, you fuckwit. He needed to buy time. If she returned he would pretend to be comatose. There would be no fun in killing him if he was out cold. She loved to taunt. A large rushing and roaring noise filled his ears. He swallowed hard and inhaled deeply – a strong odour of plastic. He squinted into the darkness. Everything was black, except for one thing. To the left of him sat a long wooden box. He shivered. It was made from what looked like old fence palings, and it was the size of a coffin. Frantically tugging at his binds, he felt the rope around his wrists loosen a little. There was hope.

Pierre felt more then heard the thud near his feet. He had been stripped of his shoes. The floor felt cool beneath his feet. The thuds became harder. Whatever it was, it was getting closer. He closed his eyes. Dropped his head. Tried to relax his trembling body. She had to think he was out. A creak sounded nearby. He opened his eyes a fraction. His attacker stood before him. They wore heavy combat boots. A long coat hung to below their knees. It had to be her. His face had been kicked with those boots. He closed his eyes and focused on controlling his breath.

"You are an evil ape. Evil apes must be punished," the voice whispered.

There was annoyance in the soft words. He wanted to ask what they meant, but it was imperative he stay silent and still. His wrists had been tied behind his back, and there was no denying the slackness in the rope. His attacker stood in front, blissfully unaware of his efforts to free himself. Without warning, a jarring, intense pain exploded in his shin as his attacker unleashed their rage. Pierre clenched his jaw and swallowed back the agony. He remained defiant. Tears stung his eyes, and he prayed they would remain concealed behind his eyelids.

His attacker huffed.

"Hear no evil, see no evil and you will speak no more evil," the voice breathed.

Pierre squeezed his eyes tightly shut as his attacker turned and walked away. Another creaking noise and he took a chance and raised his head. *Alone.* Now was the time to break free. He didn't want to die.

Speak no evil. I'll give you speak no evil you fucken bitch. I'm going to tell the world what you've done, and you're going to rot in gaol.

Fury swept through him as he clenched his jaw, his arms straining against the ropes. The pain was excruciating, but the knots began to slip. Taking a calming breath, he relaxed a moment. Cool air filled his lungs. Burning pain radiated from his wrists. A deep breath and he pulled again. And again. The rope crackled. The twine snapped.

Pierre grinned. He was free.

Bridget Tilner wouldn't know what hit her.

CHAPTER THIRTY

Daniel sat on the lounge wondering what to do. The sun was disappearing behind the horizon, and the night air was beginning to settle in. He hadn't heard back from Dr Taylor. He needed to find a replacement therapist for Bridget, and it had been two days since he had sent him the request. He wondered if he should ask another psychiatrist. The clock was ticking. Daniel wanted to tell Bridget he'd found someone suitable. He missed seeing her, and wanted to move forward with his life. He wanted to make her happy. Wanted to show her how deeply he felt.

His phone vibrated in his pocket. *Bridget.* He pressed the button. "Bridget, I was just thinking of you." He couldn't help but smile. "Are you okay?"

"Have you heard?" she asked.

"Have I heard what?"

"Everyone's going to think I did it. Zack phoned accusing me," she said, her voice panicked and raised.

"What are you talking about? Calm down and tell me."

"I can't calm down! I don't know what to do! Everything feels like its falling apart… If I do say something, if I don't say something, he's going to use it against me!"

Daniel stood and ran his hand over his face and through his hair as he walked to the window and looked outside. Why had he agreed that she go away? He wanted to hold her in his arms and tell her everything would be okay. "Where are you?"

"What do you mean? I'm in Melbourne. Where else would I be? And why are you asking me where I am? You think it too, don't you? You're just like Zack! Something happens and immediately you all point the finger at me!"

"Bridget, you need to calm down," he said as evenly as he could. "Take a few deep breathes, and tell me what's wrong."

Daniel heard her breath puffed over the line.

"He told me. Zack."

"Told you what?"

"Three employees from Wolf Industries are missing, Samuel Easton, Arthur Fuller and Pierre Rainer."

"Yes, I heard," he said calmly. "But you're in Melbourne."

"Yes. Yes, I'm in Melbourne... I told you I'm in Melbourne," Bridget said.

"Then why are you upset? Why are you saying people will blame you? If you're in Melbourne you have nothing to worry about."

"Why are you talking like that?" Bridget snapped. "Are you insinuating that I'm lying? Why are you talking like that, Daniel?"

"Talking like what? I'm not insinuating anything. You said you were going to Melbourne. I dropped you off at the airport." He stared at his reflection in the glass and ignored the worry he saw in his eyes. "You say you're in Melbourne now so you have nothing to worry about. Please Bridget, you need to calm down."

"Please don't tell me what I need to do, Daniel! I know what I have to do. I have to go."

The line went dead. "Dammit!" When he tried to call her back, she'd switched off her phone.

"Fuck!" He threw his telephone on the lounge. Why would she do that? She knew the only way he could contact her was on her mobile. And why was she acting so irrationally? He just wanted to talk to her and make sure she was safe. Why did she continue to take calls from Zack? He closed his eyes and prayed she would be okay. He wondered if finding her a new psychiatrist was a wise move.

CHAPTER THIRTY-ONE

Pierre took off headlong down the stairs. He smashed through the screen door, leapt over the front steps and onto the grass. He had expected to be blinded by the sun. He was not. The sky was dark and cloudy. He stumbled, fell to his knees, then scrambled to his feet. He dared not look back. There was no time for hesitation, no time to think, no time to plan. There was definitely no time to study his surrounds. His eyes were drawn forward to a pathway that led into dense bushland. He would disappear into the darkness. There would be no stopping his escape. He had no idea where his attacker was. Had no idea where he was going. The only thing he knew was he had to get to the path. The bushland would be his protection. The pathway would lead him to safety. *I'll run through the night.* By the morning he would be free.

He raced deeper and deeper into the shadows. The pathway began to narrow. The ground beneath his feet became uneven and rough. His vision became unclear. Before he knew it, he had taken one step off the path and then one more. The path vanished. He stopped. Confused and disorientated, he glanced around but everything appeared the same. Darkness devoured traces of where he had been. The bushes appeared alive. His skin prickled, like he was being watched. Everything was closing in. Pierre struggled for breath. He gasped desperately for air. He spun around and tried frantically to retrace his steps. It was impossible. *I'm lost!* He was lost. But he had to keep moving. He prayed he was heading the right way. He stepped forward then hesitated. What would happen if he travelled in the wrong direction? He could be heading into the hands of his attacker. The only way to escape was to create distance. Standing still would get him nowhere. Indecision would see him recaptured.

He began to move. Being silent was impossible. Leaves crunched beneath his bare feet. *Ouch! Fuck, why didn't I find my shoes.* Twigs and branches cracked. He prayed he would not be heard. Prayed he was heading in the right direction. His pace increased but running full tilt was no longer possible. A dense undergrowth, thick canopy and cloudy sky meant poor visibility. Sharp bushes began to grab and scratch his thighs. A strange whistle echoed, stopped then echoed again. He peered into the blackness as he moved. He swallowed hard. His attacker was taunting him. Pierre stopped, dropped to his knees and froze. He could see nothing. His heart pounding so loud he thought his attacker could hear it. Dampness and rotting wood assaulted his senses. The whistling returned. Footsteps seemed to come from all around him. His ears had to be playing tricks on him. Sometimes the footsteps dashed around in front, and then they would creep from behind. His attacker was tormenting him.

Panic bombarded his thoughts, and he began to question the wisdom of his actions. Why had he run into the darkness? In movies, only stupid women ran into the dark and they were always doomed. People were attacked and murdered in the dark. Why hadn't he searched for a road? Why hadn't he clung to the light? Now he was trapped in the blackness, trapped by his own stupidity.

Crickets fell silent. Twigs snapped and leaves crunched nearby. Pierre stretched out flat on his stomach within the thick undergrowth and he remained perfectly still. But he couldn't help but pop his head up slightly. He watched. He listened. His heart pounded. Time appeared to stand still.

Something brushed against his face.

His reflexes kicked in. He flinched. Whimpered. The approaching footsteps changed direction. They got closer. The pace increased. The hunt was on. The footfalls were loud and threatening, and Pierre feared he'd been seen. He needed to escape. He leapt to his feet and bolted through the bush. Branches snagged and tore at his clothes, ate into his already punished skin. The scent of his blood churned his stomach.

Sheer determination propelled him forward. He stumbled and wove his way through the bushes. He tripped and climbed over rocks, and he prayed he would see a light in the distance. But no light appeared. Fear that he was no closer to help and safety than when he had started brought a whimper to him. How much time had passed? The muscles in his legs began to burn. Scratches covered his face, arms and legs. Every part of him ached. He slowed but he would not stop. Had he lost his attacker?

No one was coming to his rescue. The only one he could rely on for his freedom was himself. *Please don't let me be running in circles.* Tree stumps, bushes, holes and rotting logs made keeping a straight line impossible. And everything looked the fucken same. The moon had disappeared behind the thick canopy. He stopped for a minute and listened. His lips were dry. His throat burned.

There was no sound of footsteps, and he breathed a sigh of relief. He had lost his attacker. Pierre continued forward in search of a light. Fine silk threads suddenly latched onto his face, and stickiness ran through his hair and over his body. He screamed; thrashed about as he collapsed to his knees. Where was the spider? His hands slapped furiously at his face. He had to get it off. The spider could be poisonous. Jumping up he continued to wipe his face. He ran his fingers through his hair. He slapped at his clothes but could find no hairy attacker. He began to calm, and stood still to catch his breath. He needed to find water. He was in desperate need of a drink—.

The footsteps returned.

Pierre took off in the opposite direction. He tripped and stumbled over a branch on the ground. His outstretched hands hit wet leaves, rocks and dirt. Damp earthiness entered his nose. He scampered to his feet, terrified he had alerted his attacker to his location. He took off again. A surge of panic welled up from deep within his gut. He stumbled blindly, heart pounding against his rib cage. The forest was full of obstacles and strange noises. His face smashed into branches, tearing his skin. Strange sounds filled his ears. He couldn't be sure where they came from. The ground beneath was lost in the muddy darkness. Branches snapped beneath his feet. Sharp unknown things stabbed and sliced his soles. His feet were wet and sore. Looking up, branches appeared as outstretched arms. The undergrowth thickened. Fear filled him.

Spatters of rain began to hit his face. Exhaustion dragged at him, and he feared he couldn't go on. The ground became slippery underfoot. He needed to rest. And while he hadn't heard his attacker for some time, they could still be close. *Hide.* That's what he needed to do. Hide and rest. He found a large log and collapsed to the ground. He smeared his face, arms and legs with mud and dirt and pulled at the thick bushes, snapping off branches, twigs and leaves – anything he could use as camouflage. He pressed his back against the rough bark and prayed no snakes lay waiting to strike. On his side he lay perfectly still, head resting on his cold and throbbing hands. He listened.

The bush was filled with incidental crackles and pops, creatures buzzed and chirped. He knew his attacker was still out there, hunting him. He huddled next to the log and hid the best he could. His attacker could be anywhere, and that induced a fear he'd never before felt.

In the darkness, rain hammered down and Pierre shivered. Maybe the rain would cover the sound of his trembling. He closed his eyes and fell asleep surrounded by the creatures in the night.

CHAPTER THIRTY-TWO

Duke Sharpe stomped up the front steps to his verandah, swearing and cursing, annoyed at his failure. He kicked off his muddy boots and yelled for his wife. Dekota followed closely behind. Both were drenched. Both were cold and hungry. They'd been buddies for over nine years – the two went everywhere together. They appreciated each other's company. Duke was somewhat of a loner; a resilient type who loved a good challenge. Besides his wife and Dekota, he didn't have any friends. Some people believed he was a little crazy, but he didn't care what people thought. Dekota was a gentle giant, protective and loyal, at times bull-headed. Duke appreciated his company. Without Dekota farming life would be extremely lonely.

Releasing a loud sigh, Duke threw his hat onto the backrest of the rocking chair and tugged at his long jacket – it was soaked and heavy. It hit the wooden floorboards with a slap. Water pooled around it. Dekota shook and watched then walked back over to the top of the stairs and peered through the pelting rain and out into the darkness.

Duke glanced at him wondering what was going through his mind. Something wasn't right. Dekota took a step back, and Duke joined him, staring out into the night. He could see nothing. The steady thrum of rain battering the corrugated roof filled his ears. He inhaled the purity in the air. Dekota lowered his head and cautiously stepped forward next to his friend. Wild wind whisked up the valley, and cold rain lashed their faces. Both retreated under the awning closer to the front door. Something was definitely out there in the dark. Duke wrapped his hand around the door handle and yanked the screen door open. He was relieved to be home. He would eat, change into dry clothes and head back out after some rest.

"Jan, can you grab us some towels," he yelled, as he stuck his head inside the door.

Dekota stood trembling to the right of him.

"Are you there Jan?"

Jan popped around the corner and appeared flustered. Her brown hair was tightly pulled back from her flushed cheeks. A bright floral apron protected her flowing pink dress. Flour covered her hands. She dashed towards the front door, fear in her eyes. Duke knew they'd been due back hours earlier.

"Oh my, what's happened? Are you okay? You're saturated! You'll catch your death," she said in a panic. "Take your clothes off… hang on, just let me clean my hands and grab you some towels."

She returned moments later with two towels then quickly retreated inside so she could serve them dinner. Duke dried himself off then limped down the hallway and flopped onto the lounge in front of the fire. Watching the flames was mesmerising. Focusing on the golden flickers, he began to calm. The warmth wrapped around his body. His stomach growled, as he inhaled the aroma of rich beef and vegetable stew. Dekota stayed outside on the verandah. His focus was still on the dark. Duke shook his head as he recalled their evening. He couldn't be bothered with Dekota. He was tired and hungry. The only thing he wanted was a nice hot meal followed by an early night to bed. Dekota ate his dinner alone. Duke ate with his wife. Both licked their bowls clean.

"I think I might have an early night," Duke said to Jan. "I have a lot to do in the morning. Dekota and I will have an early start. Have to check the pump at the dam is still working and the tractor needs an oil change. I also want to take a stroll over towards the old quarry. I'm not sure but something doesn't feel right. I think I'll take my gun tomorrow," he said, as he reached forward and placed his hands closer to the flames.

"What do you mean?" Jan asked, as she stuck her head into the lounge room.

"It's nothing to worry about," he told her. "I just think I'll take my gun, so if you hear some shooting you know it will be me."

"Oh, okay dear. Well, I'm going into town tomorrow, so I probably won't hear much of anything. I have my quilters club luncheon and I probably won't be home till near dinner time."

Duke smiled. He liked it when Jan went to town; she always bought back special treats. They had been happily married for nearly twenty years and although he wasn't a social person he knew she enjoyed her quilters club, weekly catch-ups with her friends from croquet and all the gossip her ears could absorb.

Walking into the kitchen, he gave her a gentle kiss on the cheek and said his good night. Jan was a night owl. He would be fast asleep by the time she made it to bed.

CHAPTER THIRTY-THREE

Pierre woke to a cracking noise. His body was cold, wet and aching. The ground that had appeared soft when he had taken rest, was now hard and unforgiving. His left hip ached and his legs felt stiff. Cautiously, he stuck his head up from under his covering of twigs and scanned his surrounds. He was unsure how much time had passed – it was still dark. He couldn't see any movement. Lowered his head, he closed his eyes and tried to gather his thoughts. *At least the rain has stopped.*

Lying in the dark, he questioned why everything was happening. Doubt began to peck his mind. Was he right in assuming it was Bridget Tilner? His attacker wore boots and a coat, but boots and a coat could be worn by anyone. He had screwed over so many people, and had countless enemies. But would someone hate him so much they wanted him dead? And what had happened to Samuel and Arthur? Was it their screams he'd heard? Their cries for help that had fallen silent? *Jesus. Were they dead?* Would Bridget Tilner go that far? Or, could it be someone else?

His terrifying predicament forced him to reflect over his life and the wrongs he had done. He'd used his large build to intimidate people into submissiveness. He'd threatened and bullied, harassed and harangued. Samuel Easton and Arthur Fuller had been his strongest allies, his henchmen. He'd used their support to back up his allegations. The three were united, a force to be reckoned with. What if someone had decided enough was enough?

Pierre hadn't been able to clearly identify the voice. They'd whispered. *What had they said?* Hear no evil, see no evil, and speak no evil. And they'd referred to him as an evil ape. Pierre closed his eyes and wracked his brain. Fuck. His attacker could be anyone. It was common knowledge the three friends went away for a mate's week. They also never mentioned where they went. And their week away was always at the same time of year.

Darrell Dawson immediately popped into his head. He worked with all three, and had recently threatened that he'd make them all pay. Pierre had been assigned to work on a job that would see him finish his shift later than he desired, and he hadn't wanted to miss out on his drinking time. He'd approached Darrell and asked if he wanted to swap shifts. Darrell had declined, saying if he accepted the swap, he'd have to pay additional childcare he couldn't afford. Darrell was a single dad. Arthur Fuller then spoke to Darrell, suggesting it would be in his best interest to accept the swap. Darrell stood firm and insisted he would not. In the end it didn't matter what Darrell insisted. The three attacked his work performance, threatened Darrell would lose his job if he dared cross them again.

"We're going to have a vote of no confidence," they said.

Management directed Darrell to change with Pierre. The reason behind their decision was, additional training required. Samuel Easton was the workplace-training officer. He submitted false evidence to support his claim. Darrell Dawson didn't stand a chance. It was three against one. They always won. A single person couldn't argue against the word of three. Maybe this was the payback. Darrell had requested annual leave.

Then there was Stephanie from Accounts Receivable.

Pierre had plied her with alcohol at a recent work function. He had sweet talked her and convinced her to go outside with him. He had fucked her in the car park against the cold hard metal of his car. He looked at her as just another notch on his belt. She had told Pierre that her partner had found out. She said he had forgiven her, as she had been drunk. Her partner blamed Pierre and held him responsible. Pierre had coerced her outside. Samuel Easton and Arthur Fuller had been there. They had stood as lookouts. Stephanie was upset. She insisted it wouldn't have happened if she hadn't had been so drunk. She believed her drinks had been spiked, and said her partner had threatened he would have their guts on a plate.

There were so many more people from Wolf Industries they had collectively wronged. Then there were family members.

Arthur's soon to be ex-wife could have held them responsible for Arthur's cheating. She had accused Pierre and Samuel of condoning his actions. Pierre knew she'd seen the photos, and said she would make them pay. She'd told them she wished they would all disappear off the face of the earth.

Samuel Easton's daughter Sharon was a rebellious teenager. Teenagers were resourceful. Sharon despised her father and his mateship mentality. She openly expressed feelings of hatred towards her father and his mates. She claimed Pierre and Arthur were responsible for corrupting her father, said they had a warped sense of how women should be treated. They had polluted her father's mind with ridiculous claims that males were the superior sex. She'd said she wished they all died, and claimed women no longer needed men.

Closer to home was his partner Judy. Two weeks ago she'd insisted he make her the sole beneficiary of his superannuation. Had she insisted on the change so she could kill him off and walk away a free and rich woman?

And what about the big man himself? Sitting high on the top of the capability scale was Edward Wolf, owner of Wolf Industries. Rich and powerful, the man could do just about anything he wanted. If you had money you could buy anything, even the services of a hit man. Edward openly loathed Pierre. The two had had many heated confrontations. Edward had stared Pierre in the face, had threatened he would take him out. The Union had protected his position, but the Union could only protect him so much. Maybe Edward had hired a hit man. A man of Wolf's standing didn't get where he was by being a nice guy. Could he be considered dangerous? With the three of them gone, the slate would be clean. Edward could ensure compliant replacements were hired.

Was Pierre the ultimate target? Were they all on the hit list? Or was he simply collateral damage? Tears welled in his eyes. He'd been an arsehole, a total arsehole. He was bloodied, black and blue. Where would his nightmare end? Maybe it was a case of mistaken identity or they were just in the wrong place at the wrong time. The possibilities were endless.

Chapter Thirty-Four

Duke Sharpe's eyes fluttered open. The bedroom was dark, and he could feel the warmth of his wife as she snuggled next to him. She was asleep, snoring like a wood saw. Checking the time, he couldn't afford to stay in bed. Today he was on a mission. He wiped the sleep from his eyes, stretched and yawned, then slowly pulled himself out of bed ensuring he didn't fluff the covers. He slipped his feet into his slippers and stretched again. His body ached. The timber floorboards were always cool in the morning, and as he snuck out into the hallway, he tried to avoid spots on the floor he knew would creak. Every morning he followed the same routine.

Before Jan went to bed she would ensure the kettle was full of water and his mug contained a teaspoon of coffee. All he had to do was flick on the kettle, have a shower and get dressed into the clean clothes she had laid out for him in the lounge room. Then he would sip on his coffee and place his empty mug in the sink. Clean boots would meet him at the front door, as would Dekota. Dekota was always ready and waiting.

Only this morning Dekota was missing. Duke wondered if he had wandered down to the dam. He was annoyed he hadn't waited. He crept back inside and opened his gun safe, snatching out his rifle and grabbing his ammunition. Yelling for Dekota would be ridiculous; Jan needed her rest. She had a busy day ahead. Duke was happy she would be out for the entire day. Her socialising appeared to energise her spirits.

With Jan gone, Duke would go about his business undisturbed. With his rifle over his shoulder and a torch in his hand, he headed down the dirt track towards the back of his property. It was vital he start his day early before heat filled the sky. He was pleased the rain had stopped. And he was sure he would meet up with Dekota along the way.

CHAPTER THIRTY-FIVE

A twig snapped behind the log. Pierre feared the worst. He tried to lower himself to the ground, but he could get no lower. His heart raced, and he searched through the darkness for an escape route. If he left his move too late, he could be caught.

Another snap. Closer this time. Branches and twigs cracked. Leaves crunched. Pierre swallowed hard. It had to be his attacker. He had to leave. *Now or never*. He lifted his body slightly and lent on his elbow. He pumped his fingers back and forth. They were cold and riddled with pins and needles from the weight of his resting head. He wriggled his numb feet and tried to get the blood flow to his cold and stiffened legs. He feared making a noise would alert his attacker to his exact location. *Three, two, one...* Pierre leapt to his feet and took off running as fast as he could.

The hunt was on.

Branches smacked into his face, and he held out his hands in an effort to protect his eyes. The overgrown shrubs blinded him. He staggered then fell. He struggled to his throbbing feet. It felt like he'd been running forever. But he couldn't afford to stop. His head collided with a low-lying branch, and he was knocked to the ground. Pain throbbed through his forehead, but he couldn't give up. He had come too far to give up now. Reaching out, he wrapped his bleeding hands around a rough tree trunk. Steadied himself as he forced himself back to his feet. The world spun. The trees began to close in around him. The air became thick, and Pierre struggled to breathe. He staggered towards a break in the trees, catching a glimpse of the morning sun.

Something caught his foot, and he tripped. This time his fall was unforgiving. Pierre's outstretched hands failed to grab anything, as his body hurtled down the steep slope. He tumbled for what felt like an eternity. His cries were brief as his body thumped into protruding rocks and broken branches. Half way down the earth gave way and he was sent plummeting through the air.

Bones snapped. His knee popped. His head smashed into the rocky ground with a loud thud. The air was forced from his lungs, and his left leg extended in a direction it was not supposed to go. He gasped then released an agonising scream.

Blood seeped from his ear. He could not move. A strained and heavy wheezing echoed. He was sure he was alone but strange noises and a trembling fear surrounded him. His breath became ragged. His toes went numb. A deep and aching cold filled every part of him. The world began to dim.

Sucking in dust and dirt, he saw something or someone move in the distance. But his fight was over. His body was a mass of abrasions, lacerations, contusions and shattered bones. He closed his eyes and prayed he would be rescued.

CHAPTER THIRTY-SIX

The sun was beginning to rise when Daniel's mobile phone vibrated in his pocket. He shoved his hand in to retrieve it, hoping it was Bridget. It was not. Although, it was a phone call he had been waiting for.

"Dr Taylor, thanks for getting back to me."

"Good morning Daniel, I hope I haven't caught you at a bad time. I just read your e-mail about Bridget Tilner. I have to say I'm not in the position to take on any new clients. In fact, I've had to close off my books to new clients. It seems the publicity around mental health has created an influx of people seeking help," he said.

Daniel sighed and rolled his eyes. It wasn't the response he had wanted to hear. Without a new therapist, he would not be able to move forward with Bridget.

"I understand what you're saying, Simon. Maybe we could work together on this. Maybe, I could take on one or two of your clients to free up your books. Bridget needs someone. I've been seeing her for years, but I'm just afraid I'm too close to make the progress she needs," he pleaded, as he paced.

There was only silence on the other end of the call. Daniel could hear Simon breathing on the other end of the line. He closed his eyes and prayed the man was giving his proposal great consideration. They'd known each other for years. Both had attended seminars together, and had an easy friendship.

Finally, he spoke. "I'll tell you what, let me go through my books and check my client list. I can't promise you anything, but I'll see if there's something we can work out."

"Thanks Simon, I'd really appreciate it if you could."

Daniel ended the call and hoped Simon would return with good news. He quickly dialled Bridget's number, wanting to keep her informed. Seconds later he threw his telephone. *Fuck.* Her mobile was still switched off. Why had she cut all communication? Didn't she miss him as much as he missed her? He wanted nothing more than to hold her in his arms. Nothing more than to make her happy, to make her feel safe. He couldn't do much of anything when she insisted on cutting off all communication. Why wouldn't she talk? What was she doing? Was she okay?

Daniel knew his worrying would provide no answers. He could only focus on what he had going on in his life. He had to resolve his issues so he and Bridget could move forward together. He prayed he would deliver good news upon her return.

CHAPTER THIRTY-SEVEN

Coming to, Pierre found himself in a world of pain. He had lost all sense of time. He was exhausted, aching, and hungry. How long had he been held captive? It could have been hours; it could have been days. There was no way of telling. Surrounded by darkness, he was unable to move. Piercing jolts sheared through his straightened limbs. Blood crusted in his hair. Dried blood trailed from his bulging right eyebrow over his cheek and stopped in the well of his neck. His body was a mass of cuts, scratches and bruises. Pain was his master. Slight scabs had begun to form. He didn't know where he was. All he could think about was the pain. His wrists ached. The palms of his hands burned. His lower limbs throbbed. Ragged breaths escaped his lips. Inhaling was torture on his busted ribs. He blinked furiously but his vision remained cloudy. He released an agonising groan. Instinctively, he tried to move his head, but couldn't. Cold, hard pressure enveloped his forehead. A sharp force prevented him from raising his eyebrows. It was as if his head had been bound within an undersized knit cap made of steel.

He thought he could escape, but his nightmare had just begun. He was completely pinned and encased. Trapped. The silent blackness was terrifying and all consuming. Confined and struggling for air, his chest ached. With every breath he drew in filthy, mouldy air. The stench was overpowering. With his back pressed against a cold, hard surface, his chest, ankles and wrists securely restrained, he was completely immobilised and defenceless. And terrified.

Pierre was claustrophobic. The darkness was suffocating. Engulfed by panic, his whole body began to tremble, gasping for breath his heart began to pound wildly. Tears ran down his battered cheeks as he sobbed, and through it all nausea swirled in his gut. Were these the last moments of his life?

Someone or something had been approaching, he remembered that much. He had thought he would be rescued, and had surrendered to his pain and closed his eyes. He'd made one vital error. One stupid mistake. He should never have weakened. He'd never given in before, never backed down. Why had he chosen that one moment to wane? His fear quickly turned to annoyance then anger. How could he have been so *stupid?* He gasped as he struggled to catch his breath. He was a fighter, and he would go down fighting. He grimaced as his determination returned. Thoughts of death were ridiculous; giving up was not an option. He vowed he would never weaken again. Trapped as he was, was the work of his attacker. He'd been caught, but Pierre would do anything to stay alive. He would beg and plead. He would kick and scream. He would fight for his life.

A light shone from within the darkness. Pierre struggled to see. He had to know his enemy to beat them. The light disappeared. He could not give up hope.

CHAPTER THIRTY-EIGHT

My intentions were interrupted by a noise from downstairs. Someone was in my house. How could I have been so careless as to leave the door unlocked? The footsteps became louder as they neared. There was no time to get to the door without being heard. Fear of being caught froze me in place. I dared not move. A creaking meant they'd made it to the top of the stairs. The floorboard at the end of the hallway had been loose for years. The squeak that was so annoying now rang out like a horrible alarm. Discovery was moments away. I turned towards Pierre, and lent close to his face; his eyes gave nothing away. If he'd heard the noise, he wasn't letting on. It was vital I kept him quiet. I grabbed the hunting knife from my pocket and held it in front of his face. His terrified stare met mine. I placed the razor edge against his throat.

"Make one move, make one sound and I will slice your throat so fast you won't have time to blink," I whispered. His eyes fluttered. Tears fell. He understood. Move and die. Pierre's life hinged on his ability to comply. Would he risk it against the hand of madness? Maybe, he thought this was his last chance. Would he scream or would he remain silent? While he couldn't be trusted, for now he was under my control. I turned my attention to the door handle. I could not turn to look at Pierre. My focus had to be on the door. There was an intruder inside. I had to stop the intruder. My heart raced. My jaw clenched. I had walked the hallway countless times; twenty paces, it was only twenty paces long. The heavy footsteps advanced. I began to count down.

Twenty, nineteen, eighteen… thirteen, twelve, eleven… My breathing became rapid, choked by panic, I clenched my fist. My body tensed ready to launch an attack. If I was discovered, there was no way I'd be able to let this unknown person leave. I'd come too far to turn back now.

Eight, seven, six… Silence. The footsteps stopped. Fear constricted my chest. My breaths short and shallow. The door was solid timber, and if locked, it would have been an impenetrable barrier. But I had fucked up. How could I have been so careless?

Heart racing, my gaze was locked to the door. Who was it behind it? Why had they stopped? *Come on; move if you're going to move.* What could they be doing? And why was someone in my house?

Five paces back from my door, meant they were near the bathroom, but still there was only silence. If they'd gone into the bathroom to use the toilet, I hadn't heard it flush. Why would someone enter my house, walk upstairs unannounced and go to the bathroom? There was a bathroom downstairs. Something was wrong. It was all too bizarre. I toyed with the idea of opening the door; played the scenario over in my mind. Relaxing my left hand I reached towards the handle, but I wasn't close enough. Opening the door meant removing the knife from Pierre's neck. If I did that, he could scream. And any movement from me might alert whoever was outside. And I couldn't risk being caught by whoever was outside. I was trapped.

I waited for one minute and then one minute more. The footsteps returned. Step. Pause. Step. Pause. My body tensed. *What were they doing?* Two footsteps. Pause. I waited. I was ready to slice then attack. There was no way Pierre would leave alive. He had to be punished. He was an evil ape.

One, two, three, I counted the steps… they had changed.

Retreating. They continued to recede. The floorboard squeaked. I released a loud sigh. My shoulders relaxed in relief. Removing the knife from Pierre's throat, a thin red line with a few droplets of blood showed where the razor sharp blade had sat. The front door slammed, and my knees buckled as I collapsed to the coolness of the plastic-covered floor.

I sat for a moment, and shook my head. No explanation would justify my being there in this predicament. No explaining could excuse Pierre's restrained body. I had been lucky. I gathered my thoughts, annoyed that I'd made many mistakes. Foolish mistakes. And that increased my risk of being caught.

I thought my plan had been fool proof. It was not. And now, I couldn't afford to waste any more time. Luck had been on my side this time, but the intruder could still be lurking. I pushed to my feet and glanced towards Pierre. He remained silent, and stared at me through his tears. For once he was doing as I wanted.

Enough was enough. It was time to finish what I had started.

It was time to put Pierre down.

CHAPTER THIRTY-NINE

Pierre strained to see where his attacker had gone. Silence ruled. He was alone. He listened for them as he sucked in short breaths that released as harsh rattles. Hope was fading. Mental determination could not fix broken bones. But now, he suspected something far more serious. Something life threatening. His future appeared dark. The stabbing pain in his chest and shortness of breath was likely a collapsed lung. And he could still feel the cold sting of the blade that had been pressed to his throat. Alive he might be, but his life was no longer his. He was a slave to the control of his attacker. Random thoughts swooped, Pierre clenched his hands in anger, his eyelids pulled up and sweat bit at his stare. Trembling invaded, his mouth stretched and his breath echoed. *Fuck! This is bullshit. This can't be happening!* A cold wash ran down his back. "Help! Let me out of here, please someone, anyone! Help! I'm in here! Help!" he screamed. Spittle flew as he screwed his eyes shut, and battled to catch his breath.

Bang!

Pierre's eyes sprung open, a sense of doom churned within his gut. All the while his mind raced. Shadows danced around the walls. A halo of light showed oily black soot marked walls from mounted candles. Long trails of wax ran down and pooled on the black plastic.

His attacker returned. They began to pace. Heavy footsteps circled him. He was tightly encased. Strapped. Helpless.

Lifting his gaze, his red-rimmed eyes implored his attacker for mercy. Pierre would say anything to stop the torment, to ease the excruciating pain. "Please, let me go. I won't say a word. I promise, please!" His words fell on deaf ears. He tried to analyse the room but his head pounded, distracting him. What happened? What sparked his nightmare? Who was this mad person? Pierre knew there were so many contenders, but how did they appear to know so much about him? His anguished cries for help went unanswered. It was a powerless terror from which he could not escape. His thoughts returned to the first person he had suspected. It had to be Bridget Tilner. *Fucken bitch!*

Pacing the room, his attacker appeared extremely agitated. Their identity remained concealed by a black balaclava, long jacket and heavy boots. The pacing stopped, and those cold eyes locked to his.

"Why are you doing this? I promised I wouldn't talk," Pierre said, his voice cracking under his fear.

No answer. They peered down into the wooden box, and it was clear they took pleasure in watching him tremble.

They leaned closer. "Your day of reckoning has come," they whispered, before turning and walking from sight. *My day of reckoning, who do you think you are – God.*

A tapping sound, like slow clapping. He strained to see what was making the noise and wished he hadn't.

"No… Please no! You don't have to do that… *Please.*"

Warmth filled his pants. Tears streamed from his eyes. He began to sweat as he followed the pounding metal. His attacker was relentless and unforgiving. They stepped closer. As they swung the metal claw close to his face, he felt the whoosh of air. He stared defiantly. He could feel the wetness in his pants as it cooled. He was relieved the room was darkened. No way would he let his attacker think it was a sign of weakness. *You know what? Fuck it. If I'm going to die, then I'm not going to die crying and begging. I'm going to defy you the whole fucking way, and if I can take just a little bit of satisfaction away from you, then bravo me.*

Sucking in a deep breath, he released a thunderous roar and spat. "Fuck you!"

The swinging and tapping stopped. His attacker leaned forward. Pierre could feel their warm breath. He could smell the scent of peppermint.

"Outside the rain pelted and the wind blew. What would happen next, no one knew. Your eyes filled with terror, your body now strapped. My anger is seething, with a hammer I tap. What will happen next?" his attacker whispered then laughed.

Suddenly the door thrust open. A cool burst of fresh air washed over him. A body hurtled past, tripping on the black plastic. They slid across the plastic, stopping at the feet of the masked attacker.

Even from Pierre's position, he could see the horror of the moment in this new person's eyes. Their eyes darted around the room and they scrambled back, as their mind struggled to comprehend what they saw. Shock, Pierre knew well what it looked like, and this newcomer shook with it. A room covered in black plastic; a lone wooden box that resembled a coffin. Screams shot from the box, and the intruder's mouth dropped open.

Pierre and his attacker had been caught. Neither had heard the approaching footsteps. Both were stunned. Pierre continued to scream. His prayers had been answered. The intruder and attacker locked eyes.

Pierre's attacker lunged, covering the intruder's mouth with a gloved hand. Muffled screams now met Pierre's bellowing. His attacker was losing control. He would be saved. He would be freed.

There was nothing Pierre could do but listen to the scuffle. There had been no time to recognise the floundering figure. It could be anyone. It could be Samuel or Arthur. They could have escaped. It could be the police. Or a stranger. More importantly, they could be his ticket to freedom. Hope returned. He closed his eyes and willed them to overpower his attacker. The scuffling continued.

After what appeared an eternity, the intruder was dragged from the room kicking and screaming and a sob broke from Pierre. Doomed, he was, and he felt sick to the stomach.

Hope vanished.

CHAPTER FORTY

Squeezing pressure wrapped around the waist of the intruder, as they were dragged backwards down the hallway. Feeble resistance appeared pointless. A trail of black rubber showed where their shoes scuffed the floorboards. They kicked and screamed. They tried to grab a hold of passing doorways. Nothing could prevent the pulling. The masked attacker was too strong. Before they knew it, they were at the top of the stairs. Loud repetitive thuds rang out and pain shot through their heels on each descending step. Finally, the pressure was released. They dropped to the floor. They spun around. They glared at the masked person. They straightened their clothes. They shook their head. Their face contorted. Their eyes narrowed and nostrils flared.

"What the fuck! Oh my god," they screamed, as they struggled to their feet, "you, it's you," they stuttered, "what have you done? Oh my god what have you done?"

The masked person stood frozen, legs slightly apart, hands on their hips. They were lost for words. They knew they had been caught. No explaining could excuse what had been discovered. Beyond the fear of exposure, was the fear their world was about to crumble. If they removed their mask they knew things would never be the same. But there was no hiding the truth. They had been recognised. They tugged at their black leather gloves. They removed them from their hands and flung them to the floor. They raised their trembling unclad hands. They grabbed the bottom of the balaclava and in one continuous motion, bit by bit, beyond their fear they revealed the person behind the mask. It was Daniel. The intruder was Bridget Tilner. She leapt to her feet. Her clenched fist struck his chest. He grabbed her by the shoulders and stared into her eyes. He took a deep breath and held her from within striking reach.

"What are you doing here?" he asked, as he shook her.

She yanked herself from his grasp. "What the hell are you doing? What have you done?"

"I promised you wouldn't have to worry about those bastards and you won't."

"Are you *crazy?* How did you get them here? You have to be mad," she screeched.

"I am *not* mad, and I'm not crazy either. They drove here, and I'm simply doing what needs to be done."

Bridget put her hands on her hips to stop them trembling, shook her head and closed her eyes. She released a loud sigh and stared at Daniel. Tears welled in her eyes.

"Why, why would they come here?"

"They camped here. I told you, I let people rent out my place. They've camped down by the river for the past two years," Daniel replied, defensively.

"You let them come here, when you know how I feel about them? Why… why would you do that, tell me why?"

"My mother always told me to keep my friends close and my enemy closer."

Anger burned through Bridget but she needed answers, not excuses.

"How did they get here? Where's their car? I saw no car."

"I took it back."

"You *what?* Where… where did you take it?"

"Why are you so pissed off? I said I'd look after you. I promised I'd keep you safe and that's what I've done." Daniel paused, his eyes widened as he threw up both hands. "You need to calm down. You need to understand. This is not a game any more. They were going to *kill* you, Bridget. They wanted you dead. Do you hear me? D.E.A.D. Dead. I had to stop them."

The room began to spin, and Bridget's knees buckled. "They were what?"

"They were going to kill you. Can't you see? I had to stop them. I did it for you. I love you, Bridget." Daniel said, as he took a step closer. "I had to help. You won't have to worry any more. You asked how they got here. They all came together in Pierre's ute. I had my motorbike. I drove his ute to his house. My motorbike was in the back. They were passed out from the drugs in the bottle of drink they had." Bridget held Daniel's gaze, her eyes brimming with tears. "And before you ask, no one saw me. You say I have helped you and taught you things. Well, you've taught me things too. And no, Pierre's partner Judy was out. No one saw me. I was careful. I left no evidence. No one knows they came here. No one will suspect a thing. I promised they would never hurt you and they never will."

Bridget reached for him and he wrapped his arms around her. She lowered her head to his chest and began to weep. "But where are they? I only saw a glimpse of that bastard… where's Samuel? Where's Arthur?"

"Dead."

"Dead…? You killed them?"

"I had to. Listen to me. You have to get this into your head. They were going to kill you."

Reality hit hard. *Kill me…?* Darkness crept into the edge of her vision… then her world went black.

***

Bridget went limp in Daniel's arms and he carefully

171

lowered her to the floor. He hurried to the lounge and snatched a cushion to place beneath her head. Kneeling by her side, he stroked her hair. She was precious. It was his duty to protect her from harm. He loved her.

Daniel remained by Bridget's side until she began to stir. He smiled when she rubbed her eyes, then smiled wider when she reached for him.

"What happened?" her voice was hazy.

"I think you fainted."

"I must have. I remember feeling dizzy. I was in your arms and the world began to spin. It was so strange. I could hear you, but not hear you at the same time. You sounded as if you were talking under the water." A sigh escaped her. "Tiny black dots appeared in my eyes, like little wandering bugs. I could feel you but then everything began to fade. Like I was sinking. I don't know what happened after that. My world turned black."

"It's okay. You don't have to worry. I'm here now."

Bridget nodded and smiled.

CHAPTER FORTY-ONE

Upstairs was quiet. Pierre had finally given up screaming. His aching body trembled, as hope faded into the darkness of his surrounds. Unbeknown to him, the lifeless bodies of his mates lay in the corner of the next room. Daniel had dealt with Samuel Easton and Arthur Fuller prior to Bridget's unexpected arrival. He had laid squares of black plastic on the floor forming large diamonds then wrapped each man up, delivering a few kicks as he went. Finally, he secured the packages with heavy-duty tape. It was vital they be completely concealed to prevent the escaping smell of rotting flesh. He couldn't afford to have the rancid stench of death linger within his cabin. He stood back and admired his handy work. He chuckled, as he realised how they resembled oversized spring rolls… that contained blood, bloating flesh and decomposing internal organs. He smiled. He felt no pity. No guilt. And absent were feelings of remorse. He did what he had to do to protect the woman he loved. It was kill them or they would kill her. Besides, they were evil apes who had inflicted pain. They deserved to die.

Daniel was meticulous. His mother had been a fastidious clean freak, obsessed with scrubbing and disinfectant. She had taught her son well. He had dismantled the torture contraptions he had made, and removed them from his cabin piece by piece. He stripped the plastic linings that had covered the walls and floors, and all these things he'd burned. Any trace of evidence melted, crackled and disappeared within the flames of an old rusty drum. The rooms had been rigorously cleaned, and he'd drenched his chainsaw in bleach. Besides their securely-packaged bodies, there was no trace of them having ever been there. He would dispose of the packages later.

Daniel's parents had been killed in a car accident when he was twenty-one, and he had no living relatives. The only person he had was Bridget, and he would do anything to protect her. He gently stroked her hair. He needed her to feel safe. He lay with her on the floor; he knew she was still in a state of shock, but he would always be there for her.

***

Bridget gazed into Daniel's eyes. No one had ever illustrated their love to the extent, he had. He had listened to her words, her fear. He'd heard her desperate pleas and had acted to protect. Zack was a wimp in comparison. She was glad he was no longer in her life. Zack had failed in demonstrating his love and devotion. But now… it felt wonderful to be loved. She turned and smiled at Daniel. He made her feel all warm and fuzzy. She slowly eased herself closer to his body and gently kissed him. He seemed to melt at her touch. He groaned as her hands wandered from his knees towards his groin. She knew he wanted her. She wanted him too. He had proven his love by ridding her of Samuel Easton and Arthur Fuller. He was her protector. The thought of killing Pierre Rainer together excited her. But first, she wanted to confront the arsehole who had ruined her life. She wanted to stare him in the face. She needed to tell him what she felt. Inflicting fear and pain would be pleasurable. Watching his last breath would be exhilarating.

Daniel looked towards her when she stopped her hand moving further up his leg.

"Are you okay?" he asked.

"Yes, but I need to see him."

"What? Why?" He stopped and gave her a half smile. He knew confronting Pierre would assist in closure and after closure she would be able to move forward.

"I just need to. I need him to see my face. I need to look him in the eyes. He needs to see me. I want him to know that I am no longer his victim."

Daniel nodded. He helped her to her feet then hugged her.

"Can I ask you a question before you go?" he said.

"Of course you can," she said with a smile.

"What did you do when you came upstairs earlier?"

She frowned. "Earlier? I didn't come up. I only just arrived and came right up. I was looking for you. I missed you when I was away. I wanted to apologise for turning off my mobile. I wanted to tell you—"

"Oh shit!"

"What's wrong?" Bridget said, panic starting to set in when she saw his eyes widen.

"Yes, yes I'm okay. I just thought of something. You go and do what you need to do. I'll be up soon."

He kissed her cheek and gave her a smile as she started up the stairs.

CHAPTER FORTY-TWO

Bridget's determined stride slowed as she approached the door. She began to feel sick. The thought of confronting Pierre had been much easier when she was downstairs with Daniel. Alone, her nerves began to take control. Her stomach began to churn. She swallowed hard. Her heart raced, and she leaned against the wall for support. She closed her eyes and inhaled deeply. Dammit, no person should cause her so much grief. Wiping the sweat from her brow, she willed herself forward. *I need to do this.* She was standing on the precipice of change. To move forward, she would have to release the past. Pierre Rainer terrified her. Pierre Rainer would not stop her any more. Bridget was strong and she was fearless.

She stepped forward.

The room was darker than she remembered. Standing in the doorway she allowed her eyes to adjust. Pierre's ragged breath filled the room. Sweat poured down her body as dread crept up from the pit of her stomach. *One step at a time, Bridget.*

"Who's there?" Pierre whimpered.

Bridget hesitated and glanced towards the door. She remained silent. Hearing his voice had bile burn the back of her throat. The thought of turning around and leaving the room crossed her mind, but she closed her eyes and grappled with the notion. Her anxiety peaked. *Not going to pass out, not going to pass out.* Fear demanded she retreat, and for years she had listened to that terrible voice, but it had stopped her living. Fear stripped her of her power and destroyed her destiny. It was time to fight back. Enough was enough. She took a deep breath and another step. Her nails bit into her palms as she clenched her hands. Her fear would control her no more.

She peered down into the box and gasped. Pierre was near unrecognisable. His entire body had been immobilised. Blood seeped from a large metal cap that encased his head, and dried blood covered his battered face. One eye was purple-black and swollen shut. Dirt crusted his face that was also littered with scratches. His nose was broken and bloodied. His lips dry and cracked. Bruising, blood and scratches were visible on the skin she could see. His clothes were dirty and torn, and his left knee was heavily bandaged. Wrists and ankles shackled, he looked as if he had been dragged from a battlefield. But there would be no saving Pierre, no quick and painless death for him.

Their eyes met, but she refused to look away. Time held no meaning.

Finally, he blinked.

"You," he wheezed, as a tear slipped from his eye. "You stopped my attacker."

Bridget nodded. Pierre began to cry.

"Are you going to let me go?" he asked.

Bridget shook her head then shrugged, battling to maintain her composure.

"I want to talk to you. If you give me the answers I am after, I may let you go."

Pierre swallowed hard. It was clear he didn't like being submissive. Hate shone from his eyes when he looked at her, but he nodded just the same. Bridget leant closer. The clock was ticking. It was only a matter of time before Daniel returned, and the last thing she wanted was for anyone to discover her secret.

CHAPTER FORTY-THREE

Bridget stared into Pierre's one open eye, forcing herself to ignore the haunting memories. She took and deep breath then began.

"I want you to imagine something," she said. "You enter a room and close the door behind you. Then you close the blinds. You turn out the lights. You shut your eyes." She paused and looked down at Pierre, who was glaring at her with pure hate.

"Do it," she snapped. "Amuse me. Imagine what I've just said."

Pierre closed his eyes.

"Don't peek. You are in complete darkness. Now imagine raising your arms with your fingers pointing outwards. Imagine turning yourself around while counting to one hundred. You stop. You keep your eyes closed. You attempt to walk to the door. Can you imagine it? Could you do it? Would you be left with a feeling of overwhelming confusion? Would you feel lost?" she whispered.

Pierre began to tremble. He opened his eyes, and struggled to nod. With his head securely restrained, it was a slight movement. "Probably," he sobbed.

Bridget felt heat rise to her cheeks and she glared at him. He was only telling her what he thought she wanted to hear. *Manipulative bastard.* Anger stirred from within, and she could hear the hatred in the huff of his breath. But she would not look away. The power was hers now. Rage hit like a tsunami and she spat in his face. Pierre flinched. Bridget recalled how he had spat in her face. How he had threatened and terrorised her. *Oh how the tables have turned.*

"Imagine that is how I felt daily because of you, you *bastard!* What did I ever do to deserve what you did to me? You couldn't stop at the harassment. You weren't satisfied with the bullying. You made me feel worthless and unclean. You stripped me of my pride, my security and my trust. You and those other bullying bastards shattered my faith in humanity. I want to know why," she spat again, as tears streamed down her face.

Pierre remained close-lipped. His silence infuriated her. In an instant, she launched a punch, releasing her rage. His teeth shattered, and pain enveloped her hand, but it felt good.

"Tell me *why*, you piece of shit! You low life egotistical, narcissistic dickweed. I want to know why," she screamed. "You fucken bastard from hell, tell me why! Why did you do it? You fucken raped me! I want to know why, why did you fucken rape me?" she screamed hysterically. It was as if a knife had been plunged into her chest. Her heart ripped out and cut in two. Tears poured from her eyes. She gulped for breath. She clung to the box in which Pierre was trapped. She began to violently shake the box. The wood creaked. The metal bindings rattled. Fear took root in Pierre eyes, but he clamped his lips shut, refusing to answer.

***

Daniel burst into the room, he had been standing near the door and heard everything Bridget had said. Her words had cut deep. "He … What did he do?" he roared as he charged forward.

He pushed past Bridget and lunged towards Pierre. His fist

smashed into Pierre's nose; cartilage crunched. Fresh blood exploded from Pierre's nostrils as the man screamed, but Daniel's blows were unrelenting.

Bridget stood paralysed by fear. She had not wanted Daniel to hear. No one knew the extent of Pierre's behaviour. She had been too ashamed to tell. Overwhelmed she collapsed to the floor. It was the first time she had admitted what he had done. Pierre wailed as Daniel slammed his fist again and again and again into the monster before him. He could hear Bridget howling, and from the corner of his eye saw her rocking on the floor.

***

Pierre was trapped in the realisation that his attacker was still alive and well. It was his attacker who posed a greater threat. Bridget Tilner was weak. She was a snivelling mess. Pierre believed she could be manipulated. There was still a chance. She had let him go before. He hoped beyond hope, she would again. She needed to know he would never do any wrong. He needed to sound sincere. He would express great remorse. Ask for forgiveness. Promise to make amends.

***

"I am so sorry," Bridget sobbed. "I should have told you." On all fours she reached for him. "I told you evil exists, Daniel. It lives and breathes and mingles amongst us. I told you to believe otherwise would be foolish. I told you didn't I?"

When Daniel looked at her, his heart broke. He smashed his fist into Pierre's face once more then went to her, lifting her from the floor and holding her close. She fell against his chest, shaking and sobbing. "You're safe now," he said quietly, as he stroked her hair. "Okay Bridget, you're safe.

He's never going to hurt you again."

Pierre whimpered from within the confines of the box. He could hide no more. His time was running out. "Please, I'm sorry… Please forgive me," he cried.

Bridget freed herself from Daniel's arms and crawled to the box. Daniel watched as Pierre stared towards her with mournful eyes. "I promise you I will never hurt another soul, I promise…"

"You promise today. You promise me because you have nowhere to run. You cannot hide. But what about tomorrow and the next day? What happens if you're free? A leopard never changes its spots. You'll never change. I can't trust you. I won't trust you. You're a *monster.*"

"You can trust me," Pierre begged, and Daniel scoffed. "You have my word," the monster sobbed.

Bridget shook her head as she stared into his evil eyes. Daniel remained silent, he could see the repulsion in her eyes, he knew she would not back down. There would be no pity. There would be no guilt. "You gave me your word before. You said you would stay away. Now I hear you planned to kill me. I can't risk it. I won't," she spat, and turned towards Daniel. "Kill him!" she ordered. "Make him suffer for what he did to me."

Daniel nodded and smiled, he could feel the warmth of Pierre's panting breath.

Pierre screamed.

CHAPTER FORTY-FOUR

Bridget clenched her hands into fists, as she walked away. She was sick of hearing his screaming. She went to the corner of the room and sat on the wooden chair. She glared in the direction of the box. The sidewalls hid Pierre, and she was glad. She didn't want to see him. She'd said all she needed to say. He held no power. He was no longer a threat. And he would hurt no one else.

Daniel stood next to the box and smiled at Bridget. He stepped forward, winked then nodded. Bridget dropped her head and held her face within her trembling hands. Elbows resting on her knees, her body began to shake.

Daniel could tell she was hurting. She had instructed him to kill Pierre, but he could see she was having a difficult time. He was annoyed she had turned up at his cabin. She was never supposed to be there. She was never supposed to find out what happened. His silence would protect her. He knew she needed space. She needed time to get her head around what was happening. As much as Daniel wanted Pierre dead, he did not want to make Bridget feel trapped by his actions. He had to be patient.

Bridget grappled with the notion of murder. It didn't matter who killed Pierre. She was there. Daniel was there. She was involved. Either way, both would be guilty. She stood and began to pace the room.

Did those responsible realise the pain they had inflicted? Did they care if they had destroyed a person's life? Did they think twice about the consequences of their actions and consider their behaviour had created a ripple effect from which many lives had been adversely affected? No, so why should I care about them... What goes around comes around. He deserves nothing more than a slow and agonising death.

"I need to go to the bathroom," she said.

Daniel nodded. Bridget strode into the hallway and gulped cool, fresh air. She lurched towards the bathroom. She needed to think.

Sitting on the toilet seat, she began to weep. Head in hands she sucked in a deep breath then ran her fingers through her hair. She had to pull herself together. She stood, shook her hands in an attempt to release her tension, shrugged her shoulders, stretched, then sat back down. The coolness of the cistern felt good against her back, and she focused on her breathing. While she appeared to be in an inescapable mess nothing was impossible. She'd been to hell and back: had faulted and stumbled, but she had never given up.

She closed her eyes and assessed her feelings. Why was she battling with the thought of killing? Pierre Rainer had destroyed her life. He had threatened to kill her. She had dreamt about the day her life would be rid of him. And now, she held all the power. His life was in her hands. It was simple. She would have to decide if she would be able to live with her actions? Did Pierre Rainer deserve to die? She knew he did not deserve a painless death. He needed to suffer. He had haunted her for years. When she closed her eyes she saw him. The wind carried his voice. Loud banging and crashing reminded her of his threatening tirades. He was filth. Lower than a maggot. He was an oxygen thief.

Closing her eyes she was hit with the vision of Pierre and how he had appeared within the box. His skin was punished and dry. He was dirty. She knew what he required. He required cleansing. She could boil a jug of water. She could deliver the crucial cleansing. She would rip away his clothes. Strip him of his dignity. Pour boiling water over his private parts. She would ignore his bellowing pleas to stop, just as he had ignored her pleas. And when she was done, she would walk off as if nothing had happened. Pierre would be scarred for life. Or maybe she could remove the guilty party. One strong hand. One tight grip. One fast tug. One forceful swipe. The offending party would be sliced off and thrown away. Bridget could feed it to the fire ants. She was sure fire ants loved fresh meat. She had seen a large dome-shaped mounded nest in an open area to the rear of Daniel's cabin. Or maybe they could drag Pierre kicking and screaming to the nest. They could stake his body over the large mound. They could watch the fire ants' attack. They would bite and sting. They would viciously attack. They would increase in numbers. They would swarm in the thousands. A force of tiny copper brown and reddish terminators would devour Pierre Rainer. His death would be slow and terrifying. His last breath would be agonising.

Bridget smiled. Then began to chuckle. She picked at her nails; a nervous habit she was trying to break. Relief washed over her as she rose from the toilet seat. Standing tall, she glanced at her reflection in the mirror confident the right decision had been made. There was no other option. Doubt had to be ignored. Fear had to be cast away. She inhaled the peacefulness in her decision. It was as if there was something inside her, another person completely. Moving forward was her only option. Once hunted, she would become the hunter. She would slaughter her enemy.

It was as Daniel had said, if they didn't kill Pierre she would be D.E.A.D. Dead.

An unexpected knocking hit the bathroom door. Bridget jumped. There would be no more delays.

CHAPTER FORTY-FIVE

Daniel was greeted by Bridget as she reefed the bathroom door open. He gave a half smile.

"I am okay," she blurted, before he had a chance to speak. "I just needed some space."

He took a step back and studied her. She appeared more settled than when she had left to go to the bedroom. "Are you sure?" he asked. "I don't want you to feel like you're being pressured."

Bridget nodded. "I'm positive. I just needed to think. I wanted to be sure of our next move."

Daniel took her hands in his. "You don't have to worry about a thing. I have it all worked out. I can do this alone if you want. You can leave, go home. I'll come to you when it is all over."

Bridget frowned. "I don't want to leave. I've accepted Pierre should die, even thought of ways in which we can kill him. Why should I go home now? The fun is yet to begin." She paused, laughed, messed with her hair, and raised her eyebrows. "Finally, I'll see the bastard suffer. There's no way I'm going to miss this show, not after missing the punishment you dealt to Samuel and Arthur. I am not going anywhere," she snapped, "I have some plans of my own."

Daniel huffed, rolled his eyes and shook his head. He had invested significant time and effort into his annihilation project. He did not want to give up what he thought was the ultimate revenge. "Oh, you have plans," he sighed, as he released her hands. "But my plan is ready to go."

Bridget stared at him, her eyebrows bunching up. "Okay then. We'll do it your way," she conceded. "I'm happy to be the spectator. But I am warning you, if I think your plan is dissatisfying, I have the right to tell you to stop and we'll change to one of mine."

Daniel smiled and nodded. He was relieved his project would go ahead, ecstatic Bridget would get to see his masterful design, and confident she would be pleased. He would prove his ultimate love for her. Bridget returned his smile. Daniel could see the excitement in her eyes, he was sure he would not fail.

CHAPTER FORTY-SIX

In the room, Daniel instructed Bridget to stand at the top of the box, above Pierre's head. He wanted to make sure she didn't miss a thing. He could tell she was excited. Her eyes were beaming. Her smile lit up her face. She had a spring in her step.

Pierre lay quivering in the box. He knew they were up to something. He expected they were going to kill him. He had heard them in the hallway. He had been unable to make out what they had said. He knew his situation was grim. The prospects of surviving were extremely slim. He prayed they would spare him of additional pain.

He looked up and saw a glimpse of Bridget. "Please… I beg of you. Please don't do this," Pierre sobbed softly, as tears escaped his eyes.

His face was filled with terror. Bridget glared at him with daggers and ignored his words. She focused on Daniel who remained cool, calm and collected.

"If you wrong me or the one I love, shall I not seek revenge? Let the games begin," Daniel declared. His voice echoed around the room.

"No! Please No!" Pierre bellowed.

Bridget grinned, licked her lips, and clapped her hands. She began to giggle with anticipation, "Let the games begin," she squealed.

"Let the games begin." A smiling Daniel repeated with a nod and wink.

Clenching her hands, she watched Daniel lock the door. "No interruptions." he said, raising his eyebrows. "No interruptions." Bridget repeated with a nod. He walked to the corner of the room and opened the wooden cupboard. Glancing over his shoulder he caught Bridget's stare and could tell she was curious of his plan. Bridget held her breath. Daniel removed a glass box; it resembled a small fish tank. It had four fixed glassed walls with wooden edging and one removable side. Bridget's eyebrows furrowed with confusion. She watched his every move. He carefully carried the glass box over and gently placed the open side down onto Pierre's stomach. The removable side sat facing upwards.

"A job for you my love," he smiled towards Bridget. "If you could just hold it in place."

Bridget jumped to his side. She placed her hands where he pointed. Her excitement was building. Daniel reached into the right side of the wooden box. Pierre struggled to see what he was doing. He flinched as Daniel's hand touched his side. Daniel retrieved two thin red straps that had been hiding in the darkness near the right side of Pierre's torso. He flipped them over the edge of the wooden box. Then he moved to the left of the box and completed the strap retrieval process. Bridget remained silent. Daniel retrieved two ratchet spindles from the cupboard and threaded the top right strap through two links on either side of the glass box closest to Pierre's head. He threaded the bottom right strap through links on either side of the glass box closest to Pierre's feet. The box sat perfectly across his torso. Then Daniel moved to the left side of the wooden box. He pulled the straps through both ratchet systems. He left a small slack in the straps. He grabbed the ratchets then pumped the handle. A loud repetitive clicking and clacking sound rang out. The straps became tighter. The glass box was firmly secured against Pierre's torso. Daniel closed the ratchet handle to lock it in place.

"Thank you, my precious, you have been a wonderful assistant," he smiled, as he grabbed and kissed the back of Bridget's hand. "You may resume your viewing post at the top of my torture chamber."

Bridget dashed back to the top of the wooden box.

"Please, it's not too late… please, I am begging you," Pierre begged. Daniel and Bridget ignored his words. Daniel focused on his plan; Bridget appeared enthralled by his actions. The anticipation on her face sent tingles through his body as he returned to the wardrobe. This time he retrieved what looked like a small reading lamp, with a flexible arm and red globe. He clamped the lamp onto the wooden chamber then bent the arm on the lamp so it stuck over the glass box. He plugged the lamp cord into the power point. Bridget watched with her mouth open wide. Daniel gave no clues about his intention. "I promised I will make Pierre pay for the pain he had caused." he said. Bridget nodded and held his gaze, her eyes brimming with tears. Again, he went to the cupboard. This time he picked up a cardboard box. Small holes were pierced in its sides.

***

Bridget's chest began to pound. She became tingly with anticipation. Something was inside the box. She could hear a scratching, grinding and hissing sound. She wanted to know what Daniel had planned. He was meticulous. She had always admired his attention to detail. He looked towards her, smiled then winked. She returned his smile as she watched him gently place the cardboard box on the floor then carefully remove the top off the glass case. All the while Pierre continued to scream. He continued to plead for forgiveness and beg for his release. His words meant nothing.

Daniel retrieved the cardboard box from the floor and

carefully opened the end. He tipped it over. Bridget jumped. Four large brown rats fell out and into the glass box. Daniel quickly replaced the lid. The rats scurried around searching for freedom. Daniel fumbled in his pocket and retrieved a roll of tape, which he used to tape the glass lid. The rodents were trapped. There was no way for them to escape. He turned on the power point. He adjusted the direction of the light. The red globe emitted an intense heat. Bridget could feel the burning incandescence. The rodents' natural instinct was to flee. Their glass prison was impenetrable. To escape they would have to burrow. Their claws would have to penetrate Pierre's torso.

The action commenced. The rats began to freak out. They began to scratch. They began to dig. Pierre screamed. His eyes bulged. He thrashed against his restraints. He began puffing and panting, squeezing his eyes closed.

"Let me go, fucken let me go! You bitch from hell! You fucken cunt," he spat, as his face reddened.

Bridget did not flinch at his words. Her focus was on the rats. At last they had cut through his skin. Their razor claws sliced. Her eyes darted. Her heart raced. Sickening though it was, it was also exhilarating, and she was compelled to watch. She didn't want the rats to stop. She willed them to keep going. She silently cheered as their claws ripped into his flesh – their digging and gnawing frenzied. Determined to escape the heat, the rats burrowed deeper. Their squealing and shrieking clashed with Pierre's agonising screams. She didn't care about his screams; he deserved everything he got. Daniel had excelled. She glanced up; he was fixated on the carnage within the box, his cheeks flushed, and his pupils dilated by clear pleasure.

The rats dug deeper. Bridget's eyes darted back down to the powerful show. There was no turning back. A large rushing and roaring filled her ears. She swallowed hard and inhaled deeply. Bellowing cries filled her ears. Her eyes were glued to the barbarous show. Her body stiffened. Her jaw clenched.

She grabbed the side of the box. An enormous rush burst through her body. Her hands tightened on the box.

Pierre's body began to convulse with the pain. The ferocious biting and scratching was relentless. The rats tore and ripped. They burrowed deeper. They began urinating and defecating. They gnawed into his guts. They buried into his warm flesh, trying to escape the scorching heat. Bridget stared into his pleading eyes. She wanted him to see her face. At last he was suffering. Soon Pierre Rainer would be D.E.A.D dead. The bastard would hurt no one else. He would speak no more evil. Blood gurgled in his throat and spewed from his mouth, splattering against the walls of the glass box. The brown rats were now covered in thick redness.

Pierre's eyes began to flicker. His thrashing slowed. The rats were winning. Bridget had seen enough. She could watch no more. Pierre released a heaving howl. Blood sprayed from his mouth. Bridget turned her back and calmly walked away. Daniel took her hand and walked by her side. He closed the door behind them.

Pierre would die a miserable death. He would die alone and in the dark. Outside they could hear his moans as he became weaker. He knew it was over. Struggling was futile. The end was near. His heaving breaths danced into the darkness. Blood seeped out from the torture chamber coffin. His agonising groans fell silent. Pierre Rainer was at last D.E.A.D. Dead.

CHAPTER FORTY-SEVEN

Blood. There was so much blood. Liquid crimson soaked through the base of the wooden box. It pooled on the black plastic. Around the edges it congealed. Some parts appeared thick and sticky, on others, a skin had formed. The scene was horrifying. Bridget peered into the box as Daniel removed the glass case. Euphoria surged through her rigid body. There was no doubt Pierre Rainer was well and truly dead. Sucking in a large breath, she smiled. *Freedom at last.*

Gone were all those bottled up fears that had churned from deep inside. Clenching her jaw, she began nodding. Her decision to kill was far more than just pleasing. Murdering Pierre was the ultimate release. Through violence, she was able to relieve her pain. Prolonging his suffering had given her a sense of power. She had been in control; it was Pierre who had been weak. It had been her decision whether, and how, he would live or die. Bridget had dreamed of the day she would be free and now she was. She had fantasised about getting revenge and about meeting the love of her life. Daniel had proven his ultimate love; he offered a special kind of spark. Gazing across the box towards Daniel, she felt complete bliss. Warmth. Butterflies in her stomach. Goosebumps covered her body, as she became tingly and wet. Rubbing her thighs together provided a pleasurable sensation. Chewing on her bottom lip her thoughts drifted to her next target. There was no need to stop now. Improvements were possible. With Daniel by her side, they would be unstoppable. She would right all the wrongs. Together they would snuff out all evil.

Looking down into the box she licked her lips and smiled. Seeing Pierre dead was the ultimate turn on. His abdomen had been ripped apart. The stench was gut churning. Closing her eyes, she inhaled the delectably wicked smell of success.

A strange noise snapped her back into the now. Her eyes sprung open. Fear replaced elation with the realisation that the rats had escaped. Bridget nervously scanned the room. Where the hell were the rats? She hated the things. They terrified her. They could be anywhere. The sound of scratching and scurrying feet amplified in her mind. *Focus. Focus on the job.*

Pierre's body needed to be removed and wrapped. A gnawing sound came from behind. Bridget squealed as she spun around. She slipped, in the blood, pin-wheeled her arms as her feet flew out from under her. She tumbled forward, reaching for the side of the box to stop her fall. She missed.

Her hand fell deep into the wet, tacky, mush. A sickening stench blossomed around her – blood and guts mixed with rat urine and faeces. Her hand pushed into Pierre's ruined gut. Slippery innards wrapped around her wrist. She screamed. Daniel raced to her side and pulled her to her feet. He began removing the chunks of flesh then told her to go shower. He would finish packaging Pierre.

Bridget sobbed as Daniel led her to the bathroom. Her body shook uncontrollably, and her blood-covered hands trembled. She couldn't stop crying. In the bathroom she stripped, then placed her bloodied clothes in a bag Daniel had given her. In the shower she let the water flow over her body. Her shaking eased. As she looked down her naked body, her panic returned. Blood covered the floor of the shower. She gagged. The smell of blood and innards was sickening. She snatched the soap, and lathered her body in the lavender suds. She scrubbed her body with the nailbrush, the movement becoming frenzied.

Red streaks covered her skin, and she feared she wouldn't be able to rid herself of Pierre Rainer. *Would someone be able to smell him on her?*

Daniel knocked at the door. "Bridget… are you okay?"

She turned off the water and grabbed her towel. She wiped her face then checked her hands. They were clean. Thank goodness they were clean. She smiled and released a sigh. "Yes I'm okay. I'll be out in a minute," she said as she stepped out of the shower.

"I don't mean to hassle you but we need to get a wriggle on. We need to get rid of these bodies."

"Okay."

Daniel waited at the bathroom door while she threw on fresh clothes and flung the door open.

"Sorry about that, I'm feeling much better now. So what's our next move? How are we going to get rid of their bodies?"

Daniel looked at her, his head tilted to one side as if he was deep in thought. He tapped his pointy finger against his chin and raised his eyebrows, "What do you think we should do?"

"I don't know." She paused then grinned. "Oh, yes I do."

Daniel nodded and smiled.

CHAPTER FORTY-EIGHT

The clock was ticking. They had no time to stop and rest. One by one they collected the bodies, battling to maintain a grip on the slick black plastic. They dragged and they pushed, pulled and kicked. Moving three dead weights was harder than anticipated. They slid them down the stairs, Daniel and Bridget gasping for breath as they watched the bodies thump their way down. But they couldn't rest. The new water tank was scheduled for delivery the following day.

They dropped the bodies deep into the hole. At last, they were laid to rest. Phase one was complete with no major incident. The packages had remained intact. Daniel gave Bridget a high five. Bridget wiped her brow and looked towards the bush. She thought she heard a noise, but she could see nothing. Her instincts told her otherwise. A cold shiver ran down her spine. Turning around she was alone. Daniel had vanished. Her heart began to pound. She took a few steps closer to the bush and raised her hands over her eyes. She held her breath. She focused hard. Nothing. Was her mind playing tricks? She dashed into the house.

Upstairs she remained silent, keeping her niggling worries to herself. Daniel's place was secluded. To think they were being watched was ridiculous. *It's only my mind playing tricks. Daniel will be pissed if I start losing the plot now.* She took a deep breath and focused on him. He was always a welcoming distraction. His muscles flexed, as he moved forward to phase two of the operation. He dismantled the wooden box, then asked her to fetch them both drinks. When she returned, he was dumping the now dead rats into the glass box. Blood soaked timber and the bludgeoned rats were doused in fuel and thrown into the old rusty drum outside. The bag of Bridget's bloodied clothes was tossed on top. Daniel flicked a match, and the two of them watched as flames leapt high into the air. Within seconds the evidence was disintegrating before their eyes. Moments later, the air was filled with a charred barbecue smell. Bridget nervously sipped on her drink. Her eyes continued to scan the bush.

"Anyone hungry?" Daniel joked, before he sculled his glass of water. Bridget gave a half smile and chuckled. She didn't want Daniel to sense her concern. She had to appear strong. She pushed her fears to the back of her mind and followed him to the back of the cabin. They would bury the bodies as the evidence burned.

Daniel dropped a ladder into the hole. Bridget stabilised the top as he climbed down. She peered over the edge then knelt and watched. His head was well below ground level. He dragged the bodies, and lined them next to each other.

"Are you okay? Do you think this will take long?" she asked nervously.

"Yep, I'm fine. It shouldn't take long now," he said, dusting his hands on his pants. "They'll never be found here, and they'll never hurt you again." He grinned up at her. "Don't you think they looked like three oversized spring rolls?"

"Oversized spring rolls…yeah," she replied with a shaky chuckle. Her niggling feeling had returned. She glanced over her shoulder, but saw no one.

Daniel climbed back up the ladder, grabbed a shovel and began covering the bodies with blue metal and sand from the mound that sat at the edge of the hole. The bodies slowly began to disappear beneath the mix. Daniel climbed back into the hole and spread out the fill as Bridget watched intently. She continued to glance over her shoulder.

Cover them over, I can still see them… Come on, cover them over. Quick! Hurry Up!

A cold breeze whisked across her body, like someone had just run past. "How about I give you a hand," she yelled. "I'll push the gravel and sand while you smooth it out."

"Okay."

Bridget raced to the pile, and pulled large scoops of the mix towards the edge of the hole.

"Whoa, whoa…what are you doing?" Daniel yelled. "Don't do that, you'll end up falling in. There's another shovel near the cabin. Go and grab that."

Bridget turned, spotted the shovel and ran to grab it. She knew she needed to rush. Not soon enough she was back and frantically shovelling. Within minutes her hands and back ached. But she would not stop. Daniel dodged the falling fill.

Bridget froze as an overwhelming feeling of dread swept over her. She glanced over her shoulder again, almost positive this time they were being watched. She swallowed hard and peered into the bush. Her feelings could no longer be ignored. "Daniel," she whispered. "Daniel… I think someone's watching us."

"Don't be ridiculous," he snapped. "No one's here. You're just being paranoid."

"I am *not* being paranoid. I'm sure I heard something. I'm sure something moved in the bush."

***

Suddenly, Daniel recalled his thoughts that someone had been in his house. He dropped his shovel. He flew up the ladder and peered out the hole.

"Where?" he whispered. "Don't point, just tell me quietly."

"Down towards the pathway," Bridget replied.

Daniel's eyes scanned. His mind whirled. He swallowed hard. What would he do with a fourth body? Panicked, he looked back into the hole. Two black ends protruded through the gravel and sand mix. Daniel jumped down. He frantically shovelled. It was imperative he conceal the plastic.

***

Bridget's gnawing unease continued. She was sure someone was watching from within the bush.

CHAPTER FORTY-NINE

Bridget screamed. A strange man stood behind her holding a gun.

"Bridget," Daniel yelled. "Bridget, are you okay?"

Moments later the outsider was at her side. Daniel dropped his shovel and raced part way up the ladder. Bridget saw the colour drain from his face.

"Well, well, well… who's been a busy boy," the man chuckled. "Looks like I've missed all the fun and games."

Bridget hands tightened on the shovel. Did she have enough power to knock him off his feet? If she hit him in the side of the head he could easily fall into the hole, and if he landed the way she wanted, he would snap his neck. Everything appeared as if it were happening in slow motion. Bridget steadied her stance; she'd propel her weight forward to maximise impact.

"Jesus Christ! You scared the shit out of me," Daniel said. "How are you, Duke?" he asked, as he dropped back in the hole kicking the gravel and sand.

Bridget didn't release her grip despite Daniel seeming at ease with the man, but she watched Duke closely as he moved towards the hole.

"Good…" said Duke. "I've been busy but not as busy as you, it seems," he said with chuckle.

When Duke took another step closer to the edge, Bridget

glanced into the hole. Daniel shuffled his feet; there was a small section of exposed black plastic, but she couldn't yell for him to cover it. She held her breath and hoped this stranger would not see it.

"I came over earlier," Duke said. "Couldn't find you. Seems you've been a bit preoccupied. But don't worry about old Duke. Hear no evil, see no evil, speak no evil is what I say," he said, cackling like an old witch.

***

Daniel swallowed hard. His mind whirled. Had Duke seen more than he was saying? He peered up and tried to study his face but couldn't tell. The sunlight behind his body made studying his face impossible.

"I see you've been doing a bit of digging," Duke said, as he placed his feet on the edge of the hole. He turned and smiled towards Bridget. A shiver ran down her spine. "If I had a gorgeous gal like you, I'd be keeping you a secret too."

Bridget stepped back; his breath reeked of alcohol.

"What's the matter girlie? Cat got your tongue? Don't worry, old Duke doesn't bite. Not unless you want him too." Duke chuckled again. "Let me show you how a real man works."

Before Bridget had a chance to respond Duke jumped down into the hole. He fell to his knees laughing. "Oh wow, that was deeper than I realised."

Daniel helped him to his feet then Duke began stomping around like a drunken fool. Daniel kicked the gravel then stood on a piece of the exposed black plastic.

"So it is either a huge grave or you're getting yourself a new water tank, let me guess," Duke said, as he tapped his fingers against his bottom lip. He raised his eyebrows then began to chuckle. "I know what you have been up to Danny Boy. Nothing gets passed the Duke man."

Daniel tightened his grip around his shovel; and Bridget knew Duke was in striking distance.

"Luckily I didn't come into your bedroom before. Old Dukey may have seen more than he bargained for." Duke stared up at Bridget then began laughing hysterically, slapping his leg with his hand like an old hillbilly. "I'd better stop my shit stirring before you smash me over the head and bury me here."

Daniel loosened his grip, sighed and shook his head. "You can't help yourself can you?"

"Sorry my friend, you know me. I don't get much company. I need to have a laugh. Laughing is good for the soul. No harm intended. But I did come over for a reason." Duke paused, his voice becoming serious. "Yesterday afternoon Dekota took off. Acted like a lunatic. We ended up over near the old quarry. This morning I went there and found blood. Have you seen or heard anything?"

"No mate, nothing. I only arrived this morning. Bridget didn't get here till later. She's been in Melbourne. Tank is being delivered tomorrow, so I had to get the site prepared."

"No worries. Probably a kangaroo or maybe a fox got a hold of a rabbit. Seen a few around lately."

Daniel nodded and smiled. "Yeah probably a rabbit and I tell you what, this bunny is bloody thirsty so how about we jump out and I fetch us a beer."

"Don't have to ask me twice," Duke replied, as he reached for the ladder.

Daniel sighed with relief. He followed Duke out of the hole. He turned and looked at the gravel and sand. A small portion of plastic poked through. He would get rid of Duke and return to finish the base work for his new tank. Ten more minutes would be all it required. Tomorrow a ten thousand-litre concrete water tank would be lowered into position. Samuel Easton, Arthur Fuller and Pierre Rainer would be buried forever.

Sitting on the front step Duke inhaled his beer. He rose to his feet and strolled towards the old rusty drum. Inside the flames had died down. Long timber palings still stuck out from the top. Daniel tensed. Bridget gulped. What if he noticed the blood? Duke threw his can into the fire, grabbed a paling and poked at the flames. Bridget held her breath.

"What are you burning here? Are you getting ready to toast some marshmallows?" Duke said with a drunken grin.

"No, just getting rid of some rubbish," Daniel said. "Had some old palings supporting the hole for the tank. I wish we could hang around and toast marshmallows, unfortunately, I have to get back to work tomorrow."

Daniel stood and stretched. "How about another coldie for the road," he asked.

Duke took the bait, and hobbled back towards the verandah. Daniel passed him another beer. Bridget chewed her bottom lip and picked at her nails then glanced over her shoulder. *Something isn't right.* Daniel continued to chat with Duke while she silently prayed he would just leave. Something rustled in the bushes, and she flinched. *What now?*

The bushes moved. Leaves crunched and branches cracked. This time everyone noticed. Something dark rustled in the undergrowth. Bridget's eyes widened. Her heart began to pound.

Duke rose to his feet. "Come out you bastard," he yelled.

Bridget swallowed hard—

A large black Rottweiler burst through the undergrowth and bounded into the clearing. Bridget screamed and dashed up the steps.

"Don't be alarmed, he won't hurt you," Duke said, as he turned towards Bridget. "Dekota, come here you," he snapped. The Rottweiler bolted forward with its nose to the ground.

"I don't know what has gotten into him. He's been acting all bloody crazy. Better take him home before he sniffs up all your gravel and sand."

Daniel nodded and looked at his watch. Bridget saw the look of concern on his face. It was getting late. She wanted to finish the hole and get out of there.

Duke saw him look at the time. He knew he had interrupted his work. There was nothing worse than being interrupted when you were busy working.

"I'll tell you what. Tomorrow I'll come over and make sure they put your tank in without any issues. Just a way of saying thanks for the beers. Seems you have the prep done. I'll make sure they don't damage anything."

"Thanks, Duke, I'd appreciate that. I can't be here tomorrow. That would be great."

"No worries, mate. Nothing worse than someone ruining your plans. I had a tank put in a while ago. The installer arrived. Climbed into the hole. Stuffed around. Ended up stuffing up the sidewall. I had to repair his damage before the tank could be lowered into place. I'll make sure they don't stuff you around. Do you have about a foot of clearance for the tank?"

"Yep, all measured and ready to go."

"Excellent, just tell me the time and I'll be here."

"They said they'd be here at noon."

"Noon it is," Duke said as he rose to his feet and shook Daniel's hand.

"Come on Dekota, you crazy bastard, let's go home."

Daniel and Bridget watched as man and dog disappeared down the pathway into the bush. Both released a deep sigh.

Daniel hurried back down into the hole. Bridget shovelled from above. The mound of gravel and sand disappeared. The black plastic vanished deep beneath the fill. Daniel made sure the surface was packed solid. He looked up towards Bridget.

"They're gone," he said quietly.

She nodded and smiled. Her shoulders dropped, as if all the weight she had been carrying around with her lifted. She'd be able to place the painful memories of the past behind her and move forward without the constant worry of looking over her shoulder.

Daniel's mobile vibrated in his pocket. He fumbled to retrieve it, and Bridget chuckled at him as she listened to his conversation.

"Daniel speaking… hello mate… that would be wonderful… fantastic… yep, I'll talk to you tomorrow… thanks a million." He ended the call and placed his mobile in his pocket.

"You little ripper," he said, grinning up at her. "I've got you a new therapist."

Bridget smiled.

Things were falling into place.

CHAPTER FIFTY

Loud banging rang out like repetitive gunfire. Bridget sprang up in her bed. The light on her front stoop shone brightly. The banging continued. *Who the hell is that?* She strained to focus on her bedside clock. It was just after midnight. Daniel leapt from the bed as she struggled to throw on her nightie. Raised voices replaced the banging.

"You… What are you doing here?" Zack demanded.

"Me? What the hell are you doing here? You and Bridget broke up," Daniel snapped.

Bridget finally pulled her nightie over her head and staggered out into the hallway. Daniel was blocking the front door, preventing Zack from entering.

"And you're her psychiatrist. I could have your job over this."

"You will do nothing except tell me why the hell you're here. Who do you think you are, coming here in the middle of the night?" Daniel said, anger rife in his voice. "She has nothing to say to you and I don't have to explain anything."

"I want to talk to Bridget."

"I don't care what you want," Daniel said. "You need to leave."

Bridget wiped her eyes and ran her fingers through her hair, glaring at Zack as she moved to the door.

"You need to talk to me, Bridget," Zack said when he

spotted her. "I know what you've done!"

Bridget nudged Daniel aside and stood next to him. "You need to keep your voice down," she said, as she raised her finger to her mouth in a shush gesture. "Why don't you go back to your girlfriend. I'm sure Sandra wouldn't be happy to know you've come to see me in the middle of the night."

"I'm not going anywhere, until you talk to me."

Bridget glared then turned towards Daniel, rolling her eyes before nodding. "Let him in, otherwise he's going wake up the whole neighbourhood."

Daniel released his grip on the door, and Zack stormed past, their shoulders colliding as Zack thundered down hallway to the lounge room. Bridget peered out into the darkness.

At least no one has heard.

Bridget waited for Daniel and walked with him to the lounge room. Zack stood firm with his hands on his hips. She couldn't bear to look at him, so she flopped onto the lounge and wiped her eyes. "Say what you have to say then leave."

Daniel sat next to her and took her hand as Zack glared at them both.

"I know it was you?"

"You know it was me, what?" Bridget sighed. "I'm sick of you coming over here with your accusations… What are saying I've done now?"

"The headlines of the newspaper, it's all over the news. Samuel Easton, Arthur Fuller and Pierre Rainer are missing. I know it was you."

"You're an idiot," she snapped. "Go back to Sandra and leave me alone. Come back on the weekend, get your boat and stay out of my life."

"Say what you want, but I know it was you."

"I want you to leave," Bridget said. "I haven't seen the newspaper. I haven't even been here," she said angered, rising to her feet. "Not that I have to explain anything to you, but I've been in Melbourne for the past two weeks."

Turning towards Daniel, she noticed his clenched jaw and hands balling into tight fists, she imagined he wanted to jump from the lounge and thump him. But she knew he respected her too much to cause a fight. Shaking her head she returned Zack's icy stare and stormed out of the room returning moments later empty handed.

"Fuck you, I don't have to show you any proof, I don't answer to you!" she snapped, as her fingernails bit into the palms of her hands.

"You know nothing. Why don't you telephone Tanya Stanley. You know Tanya; she and I have been friends for years. You met her several times and said how nice she was. She'll tell you I was there. She lives in Melbourne now. I went out for dinner with her while I was there. We talked about my moving there. I told her you had left me. I spoke about how I felt like a fresh start away from all the memories." Bridget paused, as she ran a hand through her hair and closed her eyes. Releasing a loud sigh, she opened her eyes and looked up at Zack, this time, with widened eyes. *I wonder if he would struggle much?* Bridget smiled as she imagined her hands wrapped around his throat. She wondered what it would take for Zack to disappear?

"I don't need to dredge up the past. I'm sick of this Zack. My life is moving forward. You need to move on with yours, and stop interfering in mine. I have Daniel now. You need to keep your accusations and threats to yourself. Daniel has done nothing wrong. He is more of a man than you will ever be. He is no longer my psychiatrist. No rules were broken. So go… just go. Your boat will be out the front on the weekend, no need to come in, just collect it and leave. I'm done," she yelled.

Zack said nothing, he glared at them both with disdain, rose from the chair and stormed up the hallway. The front door slammed. Bridget released a loud sigh and shook her head. "Why can't he just drop it? Why won't he leave me alone?" Daniel grabbed her hand and pulled her from the lounge.

"Come on, let's go back to bed. Forget about him, he can't prove a thing."

Daniel checked the front door was locked then kept a hold of Bridget's hand as they made their way back to the bedroom. Once in bed Bridget snuggled into his chest. He wrapped his arms around her. She could feel his gentle breath. She could feel the warmth of his body. She focused on the soft scent of lavender that sat in the oil burner. She closed her eyes and drifted back to sleep.

CHAPTER FIFTY-ONE

"I don't care what you think, and I certainly don't give a rat's arse if she's in tears. You both work for me and I don't do pity parties," Edward Wolf yelled. He sucked in another breath and continued. "Her dead aunt means nothing to me. If she can't get her shit together, then piss her off. Performance review her arse out of there. You know you have my support. These bitches just want to ruin our lives. Why do they even want to work in business?" He smashed his fist down on his desk. "Women are good for only two things! Fucking and fucking off. Do it!" He slammed the phone onto his office desk and peered towards his masseuse.

"Good afternoon, Mr Wolf. My—"

"Yes, yes Simon. You are here for my massage. How long should it take? I have a dinner engagement," he snapped, cutting the greeting short. The telephone rang again, and Wolf snatched at the receiver.

"What is it now?" he yelled. "I don't care what the Union says or does. I want them gone. This is my business and I'll run it how I want. It's been three months since I got rid of that bloody Pierre Rainer and those other two morons. I am not going to start this again."

He smashed the receiver down then turned his attention to his masseuse. "How long?" he said, and looked at his watch.

"I wouldn't be worried about your dinner. It will all be

over by then," his masseuse replied nervously. "If you would like to undress we can get started. I'll set the table up over here and give you a minute. Please strip down and remove all clothing and jewellery. Just leave your underwear on and lie down on the bed; face up and with the towel over your waist."

The conversation continued as Wolf de-robed. "Is there anything in particular you would like me to work on?"

"Yes, my shoulders and neck have been giving me grief. I have so many headaches I have to deal with," he snorted.

"No worries there, when I've finished with you, you won't have anything to worry about."

"Good man. That's what I like to hear."

Unfolding the table his masseuse ensured all the locking pins were in place. The last thing he wanted was for the table to collapse. He hoped it would withstand the weight. Mr Wolf had been described as a big man – he'd seen photos of him – but in real life he appeared bigger. In fact, he would have been classed as morbidly obese. Wolf reminded him of Jabba the Hutt, from *Star Wars*; a large slug-like alien, a cross between a toad and a Cheshire cat. Jabba had made him feel ill while watching Star Wars. Edward Wolf had the same effect. He was loud, abrupt, rude and obnoxious. Edward Wolf used his size to intimidate and bully. Thin-framed glasses, perched on his snub nose, highlighted his dark, soulless eyes.

Wolf kicked off his shoes. He strained to reach his socks. Undoing his belt, his trousers dropped to the floor. Loose coin jingled in his pocket.

"When my fiancée found out you were my client, she was so excited. She knows so much about you and how you built such a powerful empire. You see we only—"

Wolf scoffed. "Women, you had better watch out. Before too long she'll have you by the short and curlies."

"Not my beautiful girl, she knows exactly what she wants. We're soul mates."

"Soul mates," Wolf grunted, as he climbed onto the massage

table. "Surely you don't believe in that gobbledygook," he said, groaning as he straightened his body. "Come on then man. I don't have all day, Simon."

His masseuse slowly poured oil on his hands, shaking his head as he approached Wolf's blubbering mass. He gritted his teeth trying to shrug off his remarks. The man was arrogant, egotistical and a borderline narcissist. *You patronising prick, you can't even get my name right.*

The man was definitely morbidly obese. Fully clothed was bad enough. Undressed he was sickening. Repulsive.

"So you say your woman admires me," Wolf said, between wheezing breaths.

"Well she does know a lot about you. She said she'd like to meet you one day. You're very successful."

"Well she is right in that regard. That's because I get what I want, I always get what I want." Wolf's belly jiggled when he spoke. "The power of persuasion. The power of the almighty dollar. A push here. A shove there. A man can get anything he wants in life. Business is like war; you have to be extremely tactical. Make your enemy believe you're willing to work together and then when they least expect it wipe them out of existence. Squash them like a bug."

"Don't you think about their families? Doesn't your conscience keep you awake at night?"

"Awake…?" Wolf burst into laughter. "I sleep like a baby. My business is booming. The best thing I ever did was branch out into Asia. Cheap, those little slanty-eyed creatures are so cheap and gullible. I can make so much money and all I have to do is pay them peanuts. I love my tax-deductible business trips," he said with a moan as the masseuse's fingers dug into pale flesh. "Those young girls are quite the reward. They'll do anything. Sit here. Bend there. Suck that. Stroke this. Come to daddy. Oh, I love those girls. That's where a woman's place is, not in the bloody workplace driving us crazy. No wonder I have a fucken headache."

"Not for much longer. I'm going to fix that up for you," his masseuse replied, as he tried to focus on his job at hand.

Leaning forward he worked his fingers deep into the top of his shoulders. His pressure increased. Wolf groaned.

"What about your wife, doesn't she miss you when you go away for business?"

"Give her the plastic card. Let her shop. She wouldn't know the difference," Wolf laughed.

" Besides, I make sure I always get what I want."

"Yes well I guess if you work hard enough then people do get what they deserve, eventually. Now, if you'd like to roll over and place your face in the hole. I'll just wipe my hands and move onto your neck. It shouldn't take much longer."

"Oh, good man."

His masseuse scurried to his bag. He knew Edward Wolf lacked patience. Leaning down, he grabbed his towel and wiped away the excess oil from his hands. He glanced over his shoulder; Wolf repositioned himself with a grunt. Pale rolls of fat covered the massage table; a body that reflected years of gluttony and greed. Quickly, he removed the sterile pouch from the bag and returned to the massage table. A disposable mix of plastic and a zirconium nitride was all he needed. Edge retention and enhanced lubricity was vital. He checked the time. *I can't wait to get out of here.*

Wolf coughed and spluttered then muttered indecipherable words through the face-hole. "What was your name again? I've been calling you Simon, but he was my last masseuse," he asked as he dropped his hands down by his side.

The footsteps returned. Wolf puffed and grunted, as he struggled to clear his throat. He could see feet on the floor near his head. He felt the pressure of one palm at the top of his head. His neck tilted back. His eyes closed. He released a loud sigh.

"My name is Daniel… but you can call me Danny. Oh and I have a message for you…" he said. "Bridget Tilner said to tell you she wins."

Edward Wolf's head was yanked backwards, and with a sweeping arc, sliced cleanly. Blood gushed to the floor as Wolf's body convulsed. His arms flapped then dropped. Gurgling filled the room, getting quieter and quieter.

Silence.

CHAPTER FIFTY-TWO

Nerves began to take hold as Bridget scanned the car park. *Come on, where are you?* Closing her eyes, she wiped sweat from her brow, and began to pray as she picked at her nails. *Please, Daniel, please be okay.* Time appeared to stand still, her breathing heavy. *Why is he taking so long?* Bridget had bestowed the honour of executing Wolf upon Daniel. It was his bonus for excellence in the field, with one condition attached; he had to return with a souvenir. A small trophy would remind them of their success, and Bridget was confident he would not disappoint. It was a risk, but without risk there would be no reward, no ultimate high.

Being with Daniel was like riding a magnificent roller coaster. The initial move had been the hardest; her life shrouded by fear, the anticipation of taking that first vital step of empowerment. The sense of dread in her stomach as doubt momentarily crept in. Self-reassurance compelled her forward, positive self-talk that everything would be okay. *Click, click, click,* that treacherous climb had begun. Images of Pierre's restrained body flashed through her mind. Surrounded by the wild ocean, he had been drugged, bashed, threatened, and restrained – screaming, and fearing the unknown; an unwilling passenger, but it was her roller coaster and she was in control.

After the initial thrill of revenge things had slowed, there was a moment to breathe, and to assess – that moment at the top of the ride. Things are about to take off; you know they will but are you prepared? Hostility rises from those trapped within your ride; oh how they want to get off but there will be no escape.

Then the world falls out from under you. Gut-churning turmoil, ear piercing screams, your heart pounding as your life flings in an unexpected direction. You are catapulted forward, propelled into twists and turns, but you hang on, white-knuckled riding it. The only way is forward. Your hands ache, and nausea swirls, but you force yourself to keep your eyes open.

Bridget clenched her hands, and grit her teeth as she recalled clinging onto the wooden box. She bit back bile, her eyes wide; seduced by the power, excited by the unknown.

Before she knew it, that ride had finished, and she didn't want it to be over. She enjoyed the feeling of adrenaline surging through her veins, revelled in the tonic of invigorating terror. It was euphoric. It took her to another realm. She needed the rush; the desire for power, and the hunger for perfection. It was addictive.

Together, she and Daniel were capable of anything, of everything. They would improve the world, snuff out the evil. Her mind turned to Zack; his life posed a great threat. Threats to power were unacceptable. Then there was Suckadick; she was an adulterous slut, a poison to society. Both knew too much, their killings would be justified, the removal of cheating liars and whores would be her gift to humanity.

Opening her eyes she smiled. Her mind was set and overwhelming relief streamed through her body as she spotted Daniel. White teeth sparkled from behind his glowing smile, and her body tingled as she rubbed her thighs together. A warm rush encased her body. Licking her lips, she could only imagine the prize he would present, and the details he would disclose.

Daniel flung the passenger door open, and jumped in and dropped two gold cufflinks into Bridget's waiting palm. "You did it! You did it!" she said.

"I did it for you. I did it for us. At last the bastard's dead."

Bridget began to giggle as she wriggled around in the drivers' seat. "There were four and four did fall. Fuck them… fuck them all!" She squealed as her body shook. The result was better than she could have ever imagined. Daniel was a man of his word and Bridget loved him to the absolute core of her soul. The tenderness in his voice and the look of adoration in his eyes as he gazed into hers, there was no doubt her love was reciprocated. Together, they had beaten the odds, overcome obstacles, and accomplished all they had set out to do. They were unstoppable, a combination of charm and intelligence.

She gripped the cufflinks tight. "Why thank you, my sweet, and now it's my time to return the favour." She giggled and messed with her hair.

Daniel lent closer, his eyebrows raised as he waited for her to continue.

"Do you want to play a game?" She paused; licked her lips. "I have ropes and knives."

Daniel nodded; fire alight in his eyes. "I'd love to play a game. Who are we going to play with?"

"How about Zack and Suckadick?"

Daniel nodded again, his breathing rapid with anticipation. Placing her key into the ignition Bridget started the car and drove out of Wolf Industries car park and into a bloodied and glorious future.

"Next stop Sydney!"

TORMENT

TORMENT